ISBN 978-1-333-40817-6
PIBN 10500730

This book is a reproduction of an important historical work. Forgotten Books uses
state-of-the-art technology to digitally reconstruct the work, preserving the original format
whilst repairing imperfections present in the aged copy. In rare cases, an imperfection in
the original, such as a blemish or missing page, may be replicated in our edition. We do,
however, repair the vast majority of imperfections successfully; any imperfections that
remain are intentionally left to preserve the state of such historical works.

1 MONTH OF
FREE
READING

at
www.ForgottenBooks.com

By purchasing this book you are eligible for one month membership to ForgottenBooks.com, giving you unlimited access to our entire collection of over 1,000,000 titles via our web site and mobile apps.

To claim your free month visit:
www.forgottenbooks.com/free500730

CHEFS D'ŒUVRE

DU

ROMAN CONTEMPORAIN

REALISTS

THIS EDITION

DEDICATED TO THE HONOR OF THE

ACADÉMIE FRANÇAISE

IS LIMITED TO ONE THOUSAND NUMBERED AND REGISTERED
SETS, OF WHICH THIS IS

NUMBER———

ISSUED TO

PRISCILLA WALKER RICHARDSON

THE REALISTS

THE CARDINAL FAMILY

Chapter Two

MONSIEUR CARDINAL

———

From the coryphées' dressing-room I saw some fifteen young women come forth, and rush headlong toward me like an avalanche, chatting, laughing, shrieking, disputing, and hustling one another. I flattened myself against the wall and was saluted on the wing with a volley of: "Good evening—Hallo! there you are—What are you here for?"

THE CARDINAL FAMILY

LUDOVIC HALÉVY

OF THE ACADÉMIE FRANÇAISE

PRINTED FOR SUBSCRIBERS ONLY BY
GEORGE BARRIE & SONS, Philadelphia

THIS EDITION OF THE

CARDINAL FAMILY

HAS BEEN COMPLETELY TRANSLATED

BY

~~GEORGE B. IVES~~

THE ETCHINGS ARE BY

LOUIS MULLER

AND DRAWINGS BY

THE
CARDINAL FAMILY

I

MADAME CARDINAL

MADAME CARDINAL

In the evening of May 6, 1870, a stout lady, carelessly dressed, with an old plaid shawl over her shoulders, and huge silver spectacles on her nose, was standing perfectly still, leaning against a post in the wings at the Opéra, with her great,

Ch Leandre inv.   L Mülle

I

MADAME CARDINAL

In the evening of May 6, 1870, a stout lady, carelessly dressed, with an old plaid shawl over her shoulders, and huge silver spectacles on her nose, was standing perfectly still, leaning against a post in the wings at the Opéra, with her great, wide-open, melting eyes fixed on the stage as if in a trance. They were playing Gounod's *Faust*. The young women of the corps de ballet were dancing the waltz of the kermesse about Marguerite; and the ladies of the chorus, drawn up in line against the scenery, with arms hanging at their sides, were singing with an air of listless resignation:

> Que la valse nous entraîne !
> Faisons retentir la plaine
> Du bruit de nos chansons !
> Valsons !
> Je respire à peine !
> Ah ! quel plaisir ! etc., etc.

I approached the stout lady and tapping her from behind upon the shoulder, I said:

" Good-evening, Madame Cardinal. How goes everything ?"

" Not so bad, not so bad, thank you."

" And your daughters ?"

" The little ones are well, too."

" Do they dance to-night ?"

" Pauline does, not Virginie. Don't you see Pauline over yonder ? She has on a blue dress with white stripes."

"Pauline's getting to be very pretty, do you know it?"

"Yes, it'll be the same way with her as with Virginie; an ugly little thing up to thirteen, Virginie was, and then, all of a sudden, she began to improve."

"And improved mightily, too. She's the prettiest girl at the Opéra to-day."

"Oh! no, not the prettiest. I haven't any maternal blindness. Marie Fernot's better looking than Virginie."

"And Pauline, how old is she now?"

"She's close on fifteen."

"Fifteen! how she does grow! It seems to me I can see her still, no taller than that, among the little urchins in *Guillaume Tell*, in the air, on the bridge and up above the torrent, during the ballet."

"Yes, she's fifteen. She's in the first quadrille and she'll be a *coryphée* at the first examination, I'm almost sure. In the first place, the manager chucked her under the chin the other day as he passed, and he don't chuck everybody under the chin, you know."

"Fifteen years old! I can't realize it.—And there's nobody as yet, I hope, is there, Madame Cardinal ?"

"Oh! no, nobody, nobody! God knows it's not for lack of proposals. There have been lots of 'em after her already. First and foremost, there's that Monsieur N——, who's hardly ever out of the house, but the little one can't endure him ; and then I haven't the heart to be rough with her ; besides that isn't the part for a mother to play."

"You have a kind heart."

"Oh! as to my heart ! At all events, what's the use of being in a hurry, tell me that ? The little one will be even prettier next year than she is now."

"And what about Virginie ? Still Monsieur Paul ?"

"Monsieur Paul ? What, don't you know ? Where have you been ?"

"I am just from Russia. I have been in St. Petersburg three months."

"Sure enough, it seems like a century since we had the pleasure of seeing you. I was saying as much day before yesterday to Monsieur Cardinal.

Well, much has happened within three months.
It's all over with Monsieur Paul!"

"All over with him! why, what has happened?"

"An accident, God knows! nothing else."

"An accident! Tell me about it!"

"Gladly—but here's the end of the act. We
shall be in the way of the scene-shifters. Come
over here in this little corner at the left."

I docilely followed the respectable Madame Cardinal, and this is what she told me, in the little
corner at the left:

"Monsieur Paul, you know, had a mania for
being always on the go; he was always off some-
where or other, and one fine morning early in
February, he said to me:

"'I'm going home to Bourgogne for three days
to look after some business.'

"That same day—there's a fatality about some
things!—lo and behold a young fellow who hadn't
been to my house for weeks and months, comes to
call on us. His name is Crochard and he acts at
the Porte-Saint-Martin. Do you know him? No?
I'm not surprised at that. He only plays odds and

ends, but he's a boy with a good physique and some talent; sooner or later he'll certainly make his mark.

"Well, he comes and he says to us:

"'Will you come to the Porte-Saint-Martin to-night? I play one of the noblemen in *Lucrèce Borgia*. I have brought you four seats.'

"There was no performance at the Opéra that night and no rehearsal, so we replied:

"'That will be first-rate.'

"So we went to the play. Well! Crochard had mighty little to say; but for all that he made out to make a hit; fine voice and good delivery, and a handsome costume—all trickery, you know. For my own part, I was carried away with him:

"'Oh! how handsome he is! Oh! how well he acts!'

"Virginie never said a word. I ought to have mistrusted something, but I was stupid that night, I didn't see anything, and yet, God knows! I'm not overburdened with innocence.

"The next day, at four o'clock, I was alone with Virginie and she was mending her dancing-pumps, when the bell rang; I went to the door; it was Crochard again.

" He came in, and said :

" ' Did you enjoy yourselves ?'

" ' Did we enjoy ourselves !'

" And then we talked.

"After a quarter of an hour or so, I was obliged to go out; we were going to have company to dinner and we must have a fish. I went out; I came back; Virginie was very red and so was Crochard. I didn't remember that till later.

" The next day but one Monsieur Paul returned from Bourgogne, and while he was in the house a letter came for Virginie. I, like a fool, went into the room with the letter in my hand.

" There was Monsieur Paul in an easy-chair and Virginie standing by the hearth.

" ' Virginie,' I said, ' here's a letter for you. I don't know the writing.'

"I supposed it was some declaration or other and I knew Monsieur Paul liked to read that kind of letter; there was no reason why we shouldn't show them to him, for we had decided before that to refuse everybody else in favor of Monsieur Paul.

" But Virginie took the letter, opened it and cried :

"'Ah! it's from him!'

"What could you expect? the child said that involuntarily; and then, when she saw Monsieur Paul get up out of his chair, she gave a little shriek and fainted. The letter fell to the floor, and Monsieur Paul pounced on it. Oh! I don't blame him; in his place I'd have done the same. He read the letter at a glance, and then I saw him tranquilly pick up his hat and gloves.

"I was busy looking after Virginie, who was lying out stiff in an easy-chair.

"'Well, what's the matter?' I said to Monsieur Paul.

"'That's the matter,' he replied, handing me the letter, and he left the room. I ought to say that he sent Virginie ten thousand francs that night. Oh! yes, one must be just, and Monsieur Paul acted like a gentleman.

"You can imagine that I didn't bother about the letter. I was looking after Virginie.

"At last she opened her eyes.

"'Oh! mamma! mamma!'

"'Well, what is it?'

"'Oh! mamma! that letter—'

"'Well, what of the letter?'

"'It's from Crochard, mamma.'

"'Well, what about Crochard?'

"'Oh! if you knew, the other day—'

"'What day?'

"'While you had gone to buy the fish.'

"'Well, what happened while I went to buy the fish? what? what? what?'

"'Why, yes, mamma, yes—What do you suppose! He acted like a madman!'

"And with that, lo and behold my imbecile fainted again.

"'Come, come,' said I, 'no nonsense; it's a pity, but health comes first of all. How came you to do such a foolish thing, and what does that wretched stroller write to you?'

"Ah! my dear monsieur, he wrote things that showed that Virginie had been running after him since that crazy performance. He apologized for not coming again; he had to rehearse during the day and act at night; and he thee- and thoued her and called her 'his dove,' and his 'adored angel'—

and he ended by saying that he would be alone at his rooms on Rue de Paris, Belleville, at four o'clock the next day. Outrageous, eh? And Virginie would have had to take to bad courses for—Do you understand that?

"I gave Virginie the letter.

"'Here, read me this; he's making fun of you; and you didn't run away from him and the result is that Monsieur Paul's gone.'

"'Oh! I don't care about Monsieur Paul.'

"'More nonsense! Come, get up and walk round the room; you look like a corpse. Ah! I'd have given you a couple of good whacks, and more too, if you hadn't thought best to faint; but, I say again, health before everything! You feel better, don't you? Good. Well, now you must sit down and write to Monsieur Paul to ask his pardon.'

"'No! no! no!'

"She wouldn't give in. On the contrary, the next day she'd have liked to sneak out and go to her Crochard; but Monsieur Cardinal and I kept a sharp lookout.

"She undertook to rebel, but she got nothing by it except the two cuffs postponed from the day before; and all Crochard had to amuse him at four o'clock was a fine letter from Monsieur Cardinal.

"I can't remember all of it, but I know it began like this: 'Monsieur, an indignant father replies to your favor of the,—etc.'

"At last Crochard subsided and Virginie seemed to have given up thinking of him. Meanwhile, not a word from Monsieur Paul except the ten thousand francs. That was something, you'll say. From time to time I spoke to Virginie about writing to Monsieur Paul.

"She always answered:

"'Yes, to send back the ten thousand francs.'

"So I didn't insist. Then I had an idea of writing to Monsieur Paul myself I consulted Monsieur Cardinal, and he said:

"'There's something to be said on both sides; but, all things considered, it isn't a mother's place to interfere. No, no, I'll write myself. But don't you be afraid: I won't mention Virginie's name; it shall be a letter from man to man; I'll tell Monsieur

Paul I am very sorry that our relations should be broken off by an occurrence I had nothing to do with, etc., etc.'

"So he wrote. No reply. A month passed like that, and we were very lonesome.

"You know how it is when you're used to having company. Monsieur Cardinal was especially unhappy; he kept saying from morning till night:

"'How gloomy the house is! How much of the time we're alone!'

"He went to the café in the evening instead of staying at home with his family as he used to when Monsieur Paul used to come.

"They didn't know about the Crochard affair at the Opéra, but they saw it was all off with Monsieur Paul; so, then, naturally enough—don't you think so?—a number of gentlemen began to hang around Virginie. The one who made himself most conspicuous in that way was the Marquis Cavalcanti. Do you know him? He often speaks of you in the kindest terms.

"Virginie had nothing to say either to the marquis or any of the others. She kept her sad looks all the time, she grew thin and pale and didn't seem to have any strength at all; she couldn't stand half a minute on her toes at her morning lesson; and you know what toes she used to have—why I think she could have stood on her toes all the time.

. "'Come, my child,' I'd say to her, 'you mustn't go on like this, you must lead a different life.'

"'Oh! mamma, they bore me so, all, all of them!'

" At last she received a letter from the marquis one day and passed it over to me:

"'Here, mamma, read this.'

" It was magnificent! it was too good to be true! You'll see why in a minute.

" I said to Virginie:

"'He's a man that knows what's what; that's plain. But do you love him?'

"'Oh! mamma, love him! How do you suppose I can love him? But, on my word, he or somebody else, it's all one to me. And, do you know, as long as I've got to take someone, I'd rather take someone I don't love. It would be too hard with the others.'

"And with that she began crying again like a fountain. Would you ever have believed that, monsieur? She was still thinking of that Crochard!

"'Come, my angel, pull yourself together,' I said. 'There's no hurry. Let's not say any more about the marquis. We'll talk it over to-morrow.'

"'No, no, mamma, let's get it over with at once. He's ugly, he's absurd. I'm sure I shall never love him. He's the man for me!'

"And, touch and go! she wrote to him and gave me the letter to send.

"Faith! I was embarrassed, and, as I do in all great emergencies, I went and consulted Monsieur Cardinal.

"'It isn't proper for Virginie to write to this man whom she doesn't know,' he said; 'no, that wouldn't be proper. I'll write myself.'

"He began to write, and every now and then he'd stop and say to me:

"'This isn't a very easy letter to write, Madame Cardinal, but I'll write it all the same.'

"And he did write it, and wrote it well, too.

"Ah! I tell you, Monsieur Cardinal has lots of tact in delicate places. He never mentioned Virginie, he always deals with things, as I told you, from man to man.

"The next day the marquis arrived.

"It's always hard to break the ice at the first interview; but the marquis was very clever and very dignified and he found a roundabout way of leading up to what he had to say.

"'Well,' said he, 'how are we going to arrange our little existence?'

"I answered him:

"'Why, what are your plans, Monsieur le Marquis?'

"Then he began to tell us his plans. Horrors, downright horrors! Just fancy, he wanted to pay Monsieur Cardinal and me a little pension and set up housekeeping with Virginie in his house on Boulevard de la Reine-Hortense.

"Oh! my word! you ought to have seen Monsieur Cardinal! he was superb! A father's dignity, I tell you what!

"'Monsieur le Marquis,' said he, 'understand this: nothing can induce us to part from Virginie; and rather than let her go from here without ourselves, Madame Cardinal and I would be reconciled for the rest of our lives to the most modest fare: soup and meat and not a grain of salt with it. Besides, what is Virginie's desire? To live with her parents. She's a wise girl, and hasn't any false ideas of grandeur.'

"He was fairly started and would have gone on like that for nobody knows how long, but Virginie cut him short:

"'Papa is right, monsieur,' said she, 'we're used to living together and you mustn't try to part us.'

"'Why, just as you please, mademoiselle, just as you please, for my heart—'

"That was too much for Monsieur Cardinal! He stood up, pale with rage:

"'None of that talk before me, Monsieur le Marquis, those things don't concern me!'

"'But I must come to some understanding with mademoiselle your daughter,' the marquis replied.

"'I don't know what you mean! Besides, I have an appointment at four o'clock and I am late now. I must go, I must leave you, but with the hope that I can properly say *au revoir* and not *adieu.*

"'I most earnestly hope so, Monsieur Cardinal.'

"'Au revoir, then, Monsieur le Marquis.'

"And Monsieur Cardinal went away, without having compromised his dignity a single instant, as you see.

"As soon as Monsieur Cardinal was out of the way, the marquis and I very soon came to terms.

"As to Virginie, she never made a sound or showed any more interest than if we'd been talking about the discovery of America. It all seemed to be as indifferent to her as nothing at all; to be sure we didn't need her, for the moment.

"So it was agreed, between the marquis and me, that he should hire a large apartment, large enough for the whole of us. At first the marquis proposed to take us all into his house, but I told him Monsieur Cardinal would never agree to that; and I seized that opportunity to describe Monsieur Cardinal's character; that he was a great stickler for honor and respect and consideration before everything; that we must save appearances at any cost; that, to do that, two doors and two staircases were necessary, so that there shouldn't be any disagreeable meetings at unseasonable hours.

"The marquis understood it all as well as could be; the very next morning he began his search for apartments, and by noon they were found. That's where we're living now—Rue Pigalle. Monsieur Cardinal likes the old quarters of Paris. We are very comfortable there, and you can come and see us. Salon and dining-room in the middle; at the right, our rooms, Monsieur Cardinal's and Pauline's and mine; at the left, Virginie's and the marquis's. Two doors and two staircases. The marquis did his best to induce Monsieur Cardinal and me to take the rooms on the main staircase side; but Monsieur Cardinal refused, with his usual tact. Tact is his strong point, you know. We took the servants' staircase.

"You see how well arranged it all is; and yet, my dear monsieur, we're not as happy as you might think. There are moments when I regret Monsieur Paul. Ah! Monsieur Paul was very fond of me! He used to take me to the theatre all the time, and those nights he hired orchestra chairs for Monsieur Cardinal, who would never consent, you know, to show himself in the same box as—It's all very different with the marquis. He's forever trying to keep me away from Virginie.

"That isn't all, either. The marquis and Monsieur Cardinal don't agree upon anything—literature, politics, religious intolerance or anything else; and so they're disputing all day long. Cavalcanti has on his card: 'Honorary Chamberlain to—to—' oh! some one of the petty princes that lost their jobs after Solferino; he's against progress, and for the nobles and the priests; you see he hasn't much of a chance to agree with Monsieur Cardinal, who hasn't any love for kings or Jesuits. That's how it happens that we have such scenes, and sometimes we do have terrible ones.

"Take our dinner on Good Friday, a fortnight ago, for example—that was a drama, a real drama! In the first place, I must tell you that Monsieur Cardinal said on Holy Thursday, just to tease the marquis:

"'I suppose you'll give us a good saddle of mutton to-morrow, Madame Cardinal.'

"At that the marquis simply said to me:

"'You know, Madame Cardinal, I don't eat meat to-morrow.'

"'And I,' Monsieur Cardinal retorted, for he's always bound to have the last word, 'propose to eat a good saddle of mutton to-morrow, Good Friday!'

"The marquis didn't say anything, and it ended there. Monsieur Cardinal was fuming internally. He had meant to get up a quarrel. He likes to have the last word, but he also likes to have somebody try to take it from him, for without that, where's the pleasure?

"The next day was the famous dinner, half meat, half fish; the saddle of mutton at one end, the codfish at the other. That was certain to breed trouble. To cap the climax, just as we were sitting down to the table, Alphonse must go and put his foot in it. Alphonse is our manservant. We have a manservant now! And this is what he did. The marquis subscribes to the *Gazette de France*, Monsieur Cardinal subscribes to the *Marseillaise*. Alphonse made a mistake and handed the *Gazette de France* to Monsieur Cardinal and the *Marseillaise* to the marquis!

"' Monsieur le Marquis,' says Monsieur Cardinal, ' here's your vile *Gazette de France !*'

"' Monsieur Cardinal,' says the marquis with a smile, ' here's your delightful *Marseillaise !*'

"*Delightful !* That was sarcasm, you understand. There is nothing that irritates Monsieur Cardinal so much as sarcasm; he often says it's the Italian's weapon, and that they have a way of their own of handling it.

"After the newspapers were exchanged, there was a moment's silence ; then we began to talk, and from one thing to another finally got to the Council. At that Monsieur Cardinal blazes up like tinder and declares that all these Jesuit intrigues are outrageous, that Rome belongs to the Italians, that France hasn't any part in it, and down with the Pope, and down with the Jesuits, and long live United Italy, *et cetera, et cetera*—in fact, a long harangue, ending with the words : ' All the priests are *canaille !*'

"The marquis went on eating his codfish without a word. That was more sarcasm, his silence ! Then it occurs to me that it's my duty as a wife to back up Monsieur Cardinal, so I begins :

" ' Answer Monsieur Cardinal at once, by some-thing besides contempt. No more sarcastic silence, do you hear ?'

" At that the marquis loses patience, gets up out of his chair and says :

" ' Monsieur Cardinal,' says he, ' I beg you not to use such language, especially on such a day.'

" ' Nobody can prevent my saying what I think and all I think,' retorts Monsieur Cardinal; ' they're *canaille*, I say it again and I'll back up what I say !'

" ' Monsieur Cardinal, I forbid you to attack my religion ; I am a Catholic and there are two bishops in my family. I forbid you, do you hear ?'

" What do you think of that ? I began to lose my temper.

" ' You dare to say : " I forbid you " to Monsieur Cardinal ! when you're in his house, at his fireside, sitting at his table ! This is too much ! Look you, you make me blush for you with your religion ! For God's sake hunt up a few morals before you talk about your religion.'

" ' Morals ? what do you mean by that, Madame Cardinal ?'

"'What I mean is very soon told. Here you are, a married man, with a wife and three children, and you leave them all to vegetate in Italy to come and live at Paris with a ballet-dancer! And then you talk about your religious sentiments! No, 'pon my word, that spoils my appetite!'

"'Madame Cardinal, you go too far. I am married, that's true, but I've told you a hundred times that the marchioness wronged me first; I shouldn't be here if the marchioness hadn't wronged me first.'

"'Well, that's very flattering to Virginie, isn't it? Do you hear, Virginie? He says he wouldn't be here if the marchioness hadn't wronged him first. He insults you!'

"'I didn't insult your daughter; you did it yourself, you old lunatic!'

" Here Monsieur Cardinal rose.

"'I forbid you,' says he, 'to call my wife an old lunatic.'

"'Old witch, if you prefer.'

"'Nor that either!'

"'Old witch! And I gave the man my daughter!'

"'Your daughter! she gave herself to me for love!'

"'For love! My daughter Virginie, love such a man as you! You don't believe it! Why the fact is, that the very day before this bargain was made, Virginie consulted me, for she never does anything without consulting me; no, except Crochard, she never did anything without consulting her mother! And I told her: "Take the marquis," says I; "he's only an Italian marquis, but still he's a marquis." And Virginie replied: "That isn't what decides me, mamma," says she; "the thing that decides me is that I'm very sure I never shall love him, and so, if he leaves me some day, I shall be glad of it rather than sorry."'

"'Did you say that, Virginie?' cried the marquis.

"'Not just that, mamma has embellished it a little.'

"'No, I haven't! Before God, who hears me, I haven't changed it a bit!'

"'Don't blaspheme, Madame Cardinal,' cried the marquis.

"'I just will blaspheme if it amuses me, you old Italian wreck of a man!'

"At that the marquis calls me a strumpet; Monsieur Cardinal gets up and tries to throw a

carafe at the marquis's head; Pauline rushes out
of the room, weeping, and Virginie, half fainting,
cries: 'Papa! Mamma! Edouard!'—Edouard is the
marquis's name—and then bursts into tears, sobbing:

"'Ah! I see that we must part!'

"It was a pretty how-d'ye-do, I promise you.
Luckily, Madame Berson, the dressmaker on the
second floor, came to play a game of loto. We all
did our best to put a good face on the matter and
the marquis went away; as soon as he'd gone,
Monsieur Cardinal and I tried to say a pleasant word or two to Madame Berson, but she
saw that something was wrong, and so, as she's
a woman of tact, she left us after fifteen minutes
or so.

"Virginie, who had a fit of the sulks, takes up
the *Petit Journal* and begins to read. Thereupon
Monsieur Cardinal leads me into a corner.

"'Did you hear what Virginie said?'

"'About what?'

"'That we must part.'

"'Yes, what of it?'

"'Why, she meant that for us.'

"'For us! You're losing your wits, Monsieur Cardinal, she meant it for the marquis. Virginie, deny her father and mother! Nonsense! However, I'll show you. Dearie?'

"'Mamma.'

"'What do you suppose Monsieur Cardinal says? That you spoke about leaving us.'

"'I!'

"'Yes, that you said we must part.'

"'Oh, papa, oh! mamma, can you believe it? I was thinking of Edouard when I said that. Is it possible for me to hesitate between you and him? But, really, you did say too much to-night; why can't you let him alone on politics and religion?'

"'Because politics and religion include everything,' said Monsieur Cardinal.

"'Why, you can talk about other things.'

"'Yes, but then the conversation always lags.'

"'Oh! well, papa, have a little patience.'

"'I will, my girl, I will, but let's make peace.'

"We called Pauline back and embraced all round. My eyes were filled with tears. Then we sat down to a game of loto as cheerfully as you please.

"The marquis came home at twelve o'clock. He bowed to me and I bowed to him, all very properly; and then I went to my room with Monsieur Cardinal. I went to bed and to sleep ; but just at daybreak, toc! toc! some one taps at my door.

" 'Who's there ?'

" 'It's me, the marquis. Get up at once.

"I threw on a sack and went out. The marquis was standing there, in dressing-gown and slippers.

" 'Is Virginie sick ?'

" 'Oh! just a little indisposed.'

" 'That scene yesterday must have upset her! I'll go and get her a footbath.'

" 'Yes, a footbath; that's what she's asking for.'

"I hurried off to the kitchen, lighted the fire and began to blow it; every little while the marquis came to see if the water was boiling. At last it boiled, so I pours out the water and goes along with the footbath, through the dining-room, through the salon, and knocks at the bedroom door.

" 'It's me, open the door, I've got the footbath.'

" 'All right, give it to me.'

" 'What! give it to you ?'

"'Yes, I'll bathe her feet.'

"'What! you pretend to say that you'll bathe my daughter's feet when I'm here?'

"'I tell you that we don't need you. Leave it there!'

"'Never in this world!'

"He seized the tub but I held on. He pulled and I pulled; half the boiling water fell on his legs and he gave a yell and dropped it.

"Then I ran through the door to my Virginie.

"'Here, my angel, here's your footbath!'

"And I looked the marquis straight in the eye and said:

"'Just try to tear a mother from her daughter's arms, will you, you grinning ape! You abandon your children, but I don't abandon mine!'"

At that moment, Madame Cardinal interrupted herself and trotted off to the stage, to return in a moment holding Pauline by the ear.

"Ah! you little wretch!"

"But, mamma—"

"I tell you M. de Gallerande just kissed you over there behind a post."

Chapter One

MADAME CARDINAL

"*Then I ran through the door to my Virginie.*

"'*Here, my angel, here's your footbath!*'

"*And I looked the marquis straight in the eye and said:*

"'*Just try to tear a mother from her daughter's arms, will you, you grinning ape!*'"

"I say he didn't."

"I say he did!"

And Madame Cardinal added a hearty box on the ear to her affirmation.

The manager of the dance came running up:

"Fined, Mademoiselle Pauline, fined!"

"Fined, Monsieur Pluque, because mamma trounced me!"

"I can't fine your good mother; she doesn't draw wages; indeed, I'll do better still and fine you twice over, Mademoiselle Pauline."

"What for?" said Madame Cardinal.

"Because of your presence in the wings, Madame Cardinal; mothers aren't allowed on the stage. That's the rule."

"That's a fine moral rule; it's to prevent mothers keeping an eye on their children."

"I don't know anything about that; all I know is that your daughter will be six francs short at the end of the month."

"Oh! well," said Madame Cardinal, "we'll pay your six francs; we're above your six francs! We should be God-forsaken indeed if we didn't have someone to pay you six francs! Come, Pauline, let's go!"

After wishing me good-night:

"Ah!" said Madame Cardinal, "what a trial for a mother to have two daughters in the ballet at the Opéra!"

II

MONSIEUR CARDINAL

II

MONSIEUR CARDINAL

On the 22d of November, 1871, at nine o'clock in the evening, I was walking along one of the sixty passages that cross and recross each other in every direction in the labyrinth of structures that compose the Opéra. The monitor of the

II

MONSIEUR CARDINAL

On the 22d of November, 1871, at nine o'clock in the evening, I was walking along one of the sixty passages that cross and recross each other in every direction in the labyrinth of structures that compose the Opéra. The monitor of the

37

ballet was walking in front of me with a bell in his hand, ringing it violently and crying in a drawling tone:

"To the stage, mesdames, to the stage! the second act is beginning!"

From the coryphées' dressing-room I saw some fifteen young women come forth, and rush headlong toward me like an avalanche, chatting, laughing, shrieking, disputing, and hustling one another. I flattened myself against the wall and was saluted on the wing with a volley of: "Good evening— Hallo! there you are—What are you here for?" I respectfully made way for this charming whirlwind, and the whole frisky, mettlesome, décolleté multitude, clad in silk and satin, tripped swiftly up the stairways.

What was I there for? I knew very well. I was there in search of my venerable friend Madame Cardinal. The door of the dressing-room was left open. I looked in. Dresses were hanging, rumpled dresses and red flannel hoop petticoats on hooks against the walls. They were the chrysalides from which the glistening butterflies of the ballet of *Don*

Juan had just emerged. Three or four mothers were there, sitting on straw chairs, talking, knitting or slumbering.

I spied Madame Cardinal in a corner. Her two long white corkscrew curls made a symmetrical fringe about her patriarchal face. With her snuff-box on her knees and her spectacles upon her nose, Madame Cardinal was reading a newspaper.

I drew near. Madame Cardinal, deeply absorbed in her reading, did not see me coming. I dropped upon a little stool at her side, and I whispered quickly in her ear this simple sentence:

"Madame Cardinal, you're going to tell me Monsieur Cardinal's story."

"But Monsieur Cardinal hasn't any story."

"Oh! yes, he has, and a very interesting one: Monsieur Cardinal was a justice of the peace under the Commune, Monsieur Cardinal was arrested ——"

"Lower—lower—no one at the Opéra has any suspicion ——"

"I'll talk as low as you choose; but I want the details. Everything that concerns you interests me. As to my discretion ——"

"I know that well enough. And I am willing to tell you the story. But draw your stool nearer."

I drew my stool nearer. Madame Cardinal began:

"I must go back a little because there are chains of circumstances in life, you know. I must begin on the 4th of September. Ah! what a day that was for us, my dear monsieur! First of all, the Revolution! You can imagine that Monsieur Cardinal didn't keep out of that. He was on the Quai d'Orsay, in front of the Corps Législatif, in the front rank, against the railing. He never came home till six o'clock, worn out with shouting: 'Vive la République!' He brought home a little five franc meat-pie and a good bottle of Burgundy.

"'Madame Cardinal,' says he, 'we're going to have a nice little dinner.'

"But just as we were sitting down at the table, Monsieur Cardinal, Pauline and I, in came Virginie and the marquis—Cavalcanti; you know, my daughter's friend.—The marquis informed us that he was going to start for Italy the next day with

Virginie. He didn't propose to remain twenty-four hours in a city where the republic had been proclaimed by the *canaille*.

"At that, up jumps Monsieur Cardinal and cries :

"'I was one of the *canaille* that proclaimed the republic!' throws himself on the marquis, grabs him by the collar and shakes him like a plum-tree. My two chicks and I had all the trouble in the world to rescue the marquis from Monsieur Cardinal's hands.

"Virginie, luckily, with her tact, smoothed everything over. She explained to Monsieur Cardinal that the real reason was that the Opéra was to be closed during the siege, that she didn't want to break off her dancing and an engagement was offered her at Milan, *et cetera, et cetera.* Monsieur Cardinal cooled down.

"'I yield,' he said, 'if it is a question of the interests of art and of Virginie's future.'

"The marquis withdrew his remark about the *canaille*, and he and Monsieur Cardinal parted very good friends.

"During the siege Monsieur Cardinal was two men in one; he was the patriot who was in favor of making a sortie like a torrent, and Greek fire and reducing Paris to ashes. But, goodness! I'll tell you the whole truth—he was also the landed proprietor. Ah! that Virginie's an angel! Before she started for Italy, she made the marquis arrange things very honorably for Monsieur Cardinal and me. You can imagine that all this was negotiated direct with me so that Monsieur Cardinal's dignity didn't have to suffer.

"The day after the marquis and Virginie went away, I says to Monsieur Cardinal:

"'My dear, don't you know some good way to invest about thirty thousand francs?'

"'Thirty thousand francs! I won't ask you where you got such a sum. I don't want to know! But real estate has taken a great fall just now, on account of the present condition of things. We'll subscribe to the *Petits Affiches*.'

"A week after, we purchased a house at Batignolles, very cheap at the price we paid. And that's why Monsieur Cardinal had two minds on the subject of blowing up Paris.

"Monsieur Cardinal behaved like a hero through the siege, however. On account of his age and his rheumatics he couldn't serve in the National Guard. But he found a way to contribute to the defense of Paris all the same; he went to the clubs every night! That life suited him very well. He formed connections in the political world. He began to be a man of some importance at Batignolles. He was elected assessor two or three times, and one night when the president didn't feel very well and had to go out for a few minutes, Monsieur Cardinal took his place in the chair for those few minutes. When he came home that night he was wild with joy, and rushed into my arms, crying:

"'I presided, Madame Cardinal, I presided!'

"You know as well as I do how Trochu betrayed us to the Prussians with his famous plan. They capitulated and made peace. Monsieur Cardinal was resigned to the inevitable; but he had a real spasm of rage, when he learned that King William proposed to enter Paris. 'Pon my

word, I don't know what would have happened if
the Prussians had come to Batignolles ! I never
could have held Monsieur Cardinal. Luckily they
didn't come any further than Parc Monceau.

"However, Monsieur Cardinal never stopped
repeating :

" ' Hark ye, Madame Cardinal, Alsace and Lor-
raine and the five milliards—something must be
done about them; but let 'em look out at Bordeaux,
let 'em not lay a hand on the republic! Ah!
if they should think of laying a hand on the
republic !'

"Then the 18th of March came, and I give you
my word of honor, Monsieur Cardinal had nothing to do with it. No, indeed; I kept him under
lock and key ten days, I didn't trust myself. There
were people who advised Monsieur Cardinal to
throw himself into the movement. He wasn't a
recruit to be despised, you see. If Monsieur Cardinal had come out boldly for the Commune, he'd
have taken many of the Batignolles people with
him.

"But he didn't come out.

"Besides, I did all I could to calm him down.

"Of course, as a wife, I shared all Monsieur Cardinal's opinions; but I wasn't a wife only; I was a mother.

"I still had one daughter on my hands, and I said to myself:

"'After all, the Opéra's been closed nine months, and when will it reopen? And Pauline isn't settled, and I shall probably have hard work settling her under the republic, whereas, under the empire, to give the devil his due, that matter will take care of itself.'

"I didn't share Monsieur Cardinal's prejudices against the upper classes, you understand. In the wings at the Opéra we see society people and we can't help seeing that they have some good points. No, I don't say that to be polite to you; I really think so. I know we must have men of fashion, because, without them, what would become of our little ones, I ask you? But then, you understand, I couldn't give such reasons as that to Monsieur Cardinal; he'd have stopped me short and said:

"'Madame Cardinal, you know I don't like to go into those matters.'

"After a week I was obliged to give Monsieur Cardinal his liberty.   He promised to keep quiet.   I let him join the committee of conciliation at Batignolles.   It was splendid! They had meetings every day and sent delegates to Versailles. All that couldn't come to anything, but it had great advantages; it made Monsieur Cardinal a man of importance and kept him busy, without compromising him.

"And that wasn't all.   Monsieur Cardinal still had his Masonic business to amuse him.   It goes without saying that Monsieur Cardinal belongs to the Freemasons.   He even held some office.   He was Grand something or other of the Second Chapter of Jacques VI.   The Freemasons were up in arms.   There were three parties among 'em; some were for doing nothing at all, others proposed making pacific demonstrations, and still others wanted to come out for the Commune.   Monsieur Cardinal thought they ought not to do anything at all, that Freemasonry had no business meddling in war and politics.

"The lodge met almost every day; they fought and wrangled, and, when Monsieur Cardinal came home at night, he'd say to me:

"'Madame Cardinal, if you want to see a man that comes out strong in a debate, look at me.'

"We rubbed along that way for a month, and, I promise you, if Monsieur Cardinal leaned in either direction, it was in the direction of Versailles and not of the Commune. In the first place you can imagine that he wasn't satisfied with the decree of the Commune about rents. The house we'd bought at Batignolles paid us very well, but our tenants, when they felt inclined, just decamped without paying, under the protection of the National Guard. And then Monsieur Cardinal's very fond of the two little ones. It was very sad not to have seen Virginie for eight months, and he knew very well the marquis wouldn't bring us back our child as long as there was a Commune in Paris.

"For my part, I became a downright Versaillaise. To be sure the Commune was talking about reopening the Opéra, but the Opéra without a ballet!

Pauline's future worried me terribly, and I couldn't keep from saying to myself:

"'I don't care; if the empire had lasted two or three years longer, Pauline would be provided for to-day, and her position would probably be assured in every respect.'

"I ask your pardon for being so tiresome, but when a mother gets on the subject of her daughter, you know, her heart runs away with her.

"Now I come to April 28th—the awful day!— the day that caused all our misery. For a week, shells had been falling now and then in the Batignolles neighborhood, and Monsieur Cardinal used to go and look at his house every morning. On the 26th of April, about eleven o'clock, Monsieur Cardinal came home with his eyes bulging out of his head and his teeth chattering in his mouth.

"'Madame Cardinal,' says he, 'do you know what's happened, Madame Cardinal?'

"'No, Monsieur Cardinal, but you frighten me.'

"'Well! Monsieur Thiers has bombarded us! Yes, Monsieur Thiers is doing what Monsieur de Bismarck didn't do! Not a single Prussian shell fell in Batignolles, and last night a Versailles bomb went through our roof. I shall have to pay out at least fifteen hundred francs for repairs!'

"I made Monsieur Cardinal take a little mint-water, and tried to calm him; but he was thoroughly exasperated, and all of a sudden he cries out:

"' I didn't mean to go to the Masonic demonstration to-morrow, but I will go, Madame Cardinal, in the front row, and offer my breast to the cannon-balls of Versailles. My hat, give me my hat! There's a meeting of the lodge at noon. I am going to join my brothers.'

"In spite of my tears and shrieks, he left the house. A great demonstration was announced for the next day. They proposed to plant the Masonic banners on the ramparts, and if a shot touched 'em, the Masons took an oath to march against the Versaillais. Monsieur Cardinal had fought the plan only the day before; but then he hadn't been bombarded! It makes a great change in a man's ideas, to receive a bomb in his roof that does fifteen hundred francs' worth of damage.

"Monsieur Cardinal came home at four o'clock. He was calm and serious and had a great staff in his hand.

"'Madame Cardinal,' says he, 'fix it any way you can, but I must have a Masonic banner to-morrow morning at eight o'clock or quarter past. I am to carry a banner, and I have undertaken to furnish it, because, you understand, the more banners there are, the more imposing it will be and the more likely to bring the man that's bombarding us to his senses! Here's the staff for the banner!'

"I saw at once from Monsieur Cardinal's tone and expression that there was no use arguing with him. Pauline and I had to go to work right away; and we made a banner that really did very well indeed out of an old ball-dress of Virginie's. I sacrificed one of my petticoats and put a layer of flannel between the two thicknesses of silk. That made the banner stiff. But the most successful thing about it was the emblems and the motto. I cut out a triangle, a square, a hammer and all the letters for the inscription: *Aimez-vous les uns les*

autres—Love one another—from a piece of blue satin
that came from an old dress of Virginie's. And
then I sewed 'em all on the white silk. I tell you,
that made a fine effect! And when Monsieur
Cardinal went away at half-past eight in an open
cabriolet, with his banner waving in the air, there
was a shout of admiration in Batignolles.

"Before he got into the carriage, Monsieur Cardinal kissed me, right on the sidewalk before a
crowd of two or three hundred people. I wept and
shrieked and clung to his coat.

"'Monsieur Cardinal,' says I, 'I don't want to
leave you! You are going into danger, I am your
wife, and it is my duty to share it!'

"But he replied:

"'No, no, Madame Cardinal, I won't take you.
I need all my strength, you might make me weak.
Adieu! Let me go! I go to offer my breast to the
cannon-balls of the Versaillais! My breast after
my roof!'

"With that he kisses me, jumps into his carriage,
bows to the crowd and drives away; and I, with
my blood in a fever, almost fainting, in the arms of

Madame Canivet, a friend of ours, a box-keeper at the Opéra, watched the carriage and the banner waving above Monsieur Cardinal's head. Everybody congratulated me on my banner.

"'It will be the best one there,' they said, 'it will be the best!'

"But you can imagine that I hadn't any head to receive congratulations.

"The cabriolet hadn't turned the corner of the street before I thought to myself: 'He wouldn't let me go with him, but I have a right to go and see him ride along the boulevard. Yes, I must show Pauline that sight, the child must always remember it. She must see her father in the procession!' Then I instantly thought of Monsieur le Comte de Glayeul, who has always shown a great deal of interest in my little ones. I had taken Virginie to his house two or three times, and he used to be always saying to me before the 4th September: 'Bring Pauline to me one of these mornings.' And you know Monsieur de Glayeul isn't one of the clowns that only want to ruin our daughters. No, he's a serious-minded man such as a mother can trust her daughter to; he's a man who knows all about the ballet and all about life; he never gave Virginie anything but good advice. So I says to myself: 'I'll just take Pauline to him. He lives on the entresol, front, on Boulevard de la Madeleine. That will do our business and we'll be in the front boxes to see the demonstration pass.'

"Monsieur de Glayeul received Pauline with open arms. He seated me in a big easy-chair in front of one of the salon windows, and sat at the other window himself with Pauline, because three at one window would have been too many, we should have been in each other's way. At one o'clock the procession began to go by. Well, now, I tell you, anybody that didn't see that, never saw anything! It was superb!

"First came the members of the Commune with their scarfs round their waists, then three companies of Turcos employed by the Commune, then the Masonic deputations, and then the dignitaries, and among the dignitaries Monsieur Cardinal, with his face beaming all over, carrying my banner. I leaned out of the window and cried to the little one :

"'Pauline! Pauline! See, there's your father!'

"But look as I would I couldn't see the little one, and I kept on crying :

"'Pauline, what ever are you doing? I tell you, there goes your father!'

"At last she heard me and leaned out of the window; she was all red with excitement, poor child, and I said to her:

"'Wave your handkerchief, Pauline, wave your handkerchief.'

"With that we both waved our handkerchiefs, and I shouted at the top of my voice :

"'Monsieur Cardinal! Monsieur Cardinal! we're up here—in the entresol!'

"He heard me and turned his head, dipped his banner a little to us and passed on !

"When I started to go home with Pauline, Monsieur de Glayeul says:

"'Oh! leave the little one with me, I'll bring her home to-night after dinner.'

"But I replied:

"'No, no, Monsieur le Comte, not to-day: I can't be separated from my child when Monsieur Cardinal is in such danger. Some other day, as long as you choose!'

"And I took Pauline away with me.

"We went home. It may have been about three o'clock. The cannonading had ceased and that comforted me a bit. But about four I heard five or six shots. I had a presentiment. I cried out:

"'Ah! that's Monsieur Thiers firing on Monsieur Cardinal!'

"I wasn't mistaken.

"At six o'clock the door opened with a bang; and Monsieur Cardinal appeared, beside himself with excitement, no hat, wild-eyed, all white with dust. Do you not know what had happened? A Versailles shell came straight for Monsieur Cardinal while he was setting up his banner between Porte Maillot and Porte Dauphine.

"Monsieur Cardinal went to bed in a high fever and, for more than a week, I was very uneasy about him. He was delirious every night and kept repeating the same things over and over.

"'Monsieur Thiers the bombarder! Shells at my house! Shells at me! Vive la Commune!'

"When Monsieur Cardinal was up and about again, about May 15th, I couldn't prevent him from throwing himself into the movement all over. They offered him his choice between a place in the War Department and a seat in the magistracy. I urged him to decide for the magistracy. It seemed to me that it was less dangerous, more honorable and better adapted to Monsieur Cardinal's character. Friday, May 19th, the *Official* published the decree appointing Monsieur Cardinal justice of the peace. I was very uneasy, but I must confess, for all that, that I was flattered to see Monsieur Cardinal's name spread out on the first page of the *Official*. Monsieur Cardinal was to have his first audience on the following Monday at nine o'clock.

"The day before, Sunday, he went and had his photograph taken in two positions: in the first he was alone, with a sober, thoughtful face, in his judge's gown, leaning against a pillar and holding the *Official* of the 19th in his hand—that was the magistrate! In the other he was still in his judge's gown, but he wasn't alone; I was leaning on his arm, he was showing me the *Official* of the 19th, and smiling at me—that was the husband!

"Monday morning, at nine o'clock, Monsieur Cardinal, in his gown, took his seat as a judge on the bench; he had such an air of authority and dignity, that you would have thought he'd done nothing else all his life. Naturally, I took Pauline to look on. The first case was called—but just as the plaintiff was coming forward, a soldier of the Commune rushed into the court-room, shouting:

"'The enemy's inside the walls! Everybody to the barricades!'

"I gave one leap to the platform. I tore off Monsieur Cardinal's gown, threw his judge's cap into a corner and dragged him home as fast as I could go. There I locked him up, and for six weeks he never put his nose outside the door. After six weeks had gone by, I was beginning to breathe again, when, one morning—it was July 3rd,—somebody rang the bell, Pauline went to the door, and came tearing back in terror, shrieking:

"'Mamma, mamma, it's the police!'

"And so it was the police. They showed Monsieur Cardinal the photograph he was idiot enough to have taken the very day of the entry of the Versaillais. Monsieur Cardinal was admirable.

"'I'm your man,' he said, 'I'm ready to go with you, I have sacrificed my life. I won't try to redeem my life by cowardice. Allow me to embrace my wife and I am at your service.'

"He opened his arms. I rushed into them and he said to me rapidly, in a low voice:

"'The marquis is the only man who can get me out of this scrape. I remember now. He was very intimate with Monsieur Thiers. He used to dine with him in Place Saint-Georges.'

"Then he drew himself up, turned to the commissioner of police and said:

"'Forward, monsieur, forward!'

"I immediately sent a telegraphic dispatch to Virginie:

"'*Your father's in limbo. Come with the marquis. He only can save us.*'

"Well, to do him justice, the marquis is a real gentleman. In forty-eight hours he was in Paris, and when I said:

"'How good you were to come!'

"'Don't thank me,' says he, 'I had to see Monsieur Thiers about Roman affairs. I'll speak to him about Monsieur Cardinal at the same time.'

"The next day Monsieur Cardinal was restored to me."

At that moment the coryphées, flowers and butterflies came rushing madly into the dressing-room.

Pauline came and stood in front of Madame Cardinal, and said, exultantly:

"Look, mamma, see the two little diamonds in my ears; Monsieur de Glayeul brought them to me to-night."

Madame Cardinal hastily replaced her spectacles on her nose, scrutinized the two little diamonds, and was, apparently, satisfied with what she saw; for she turned to me and said:

"He behaves very handsomely to Pauline, does Monsieur de Glayeul. Do you know it was an inspiration from Heaven, my going to his house the day of Monsieur Cardinal's demonstration. And now go, you. You're in the way here. These children are too well brought up to undress before you."

III

THE LITTLE CARDINALS

III

THE LITTLE CARDINALS

III

THE LITTLE CARDINALS

It was November 29, 1875, the evening of the reproduction of *Don Juan* at the Opéra. The second act was being sung. I had an orchestra chair on the right, in a little corner occupied by old habitués who *listen* to nothing but the ballet.

63

Ch Léandre inv.   L.Müller sc.

III

THE LITTLE CARDINALS

It was November 29, 1875, the evening of the reproduction of *Don Juan* at the Opéra. The second act was being sung. I had an orchestra chair on the right, in a little corner occupied by old habitués who *listen* to nothing but the ballet.

63

And as the ballet did not come on until the following act, but little attention was being paid, in that particular corner, to the quarrel between Zerlina and Masetto. We were talking and joking. We were speaking of old times, of the old opera-house on Rue Le Peletier, of the Opéra before the war and before the fire. What irreparable losses in the corps de ballet! How many pretty girls had disappeared! The Villeroys, the Brachs, the Volters, the Georgeaults,—and the little Cardinals.

The little Cardinals! I had forgotten them. The little Cardinals, everlastingly flanked by their venerable mother, the majestic, the massive Madame Cardinal, with her imposing crown of white hair, with her beautiful silver spectacles planted upon a huge nose all black with snuff. And Monsieur Cardinal!—I knew nothing whatever of the present circumstances of that interesting family. It seemed to me a favorable opportunity to find out something about them.

When the curtain fell I went behind the scenes. Behold me in the dancers' greenroom, just before the ballet divertissement, patiently beginning my little quest. I question the old employés of the Opéra. The reply is always the same:

"Virginie Cardinal never came back to the Opéra after the war, and Pauline Cardinal hasn't been seen since the fire."

No more little Cardinals! no more Madame Cardinal!

The chain was broken.

The individuals I questioned listened to me absent-mindedly. It was not only the first performance of *Don Juan*, but the first appearance of Grevin's costumes, and the young women were assuming pretty postures before the great mirror in the greenroom, tightening the laces of their dancing-pumps, swelling out in a way to burst their clothes, and arranging their clouds of gauze.

Suddenly, borr! borr! sounded sharply the electric bell.

"Stage! stage!"

General exit.

The whole army of Pierrettes, Polichinelles and Arlequines drew up in good order, at the rear of the stage, upon a great platform.

They awaited there the signal for the grand
march, and, elevated as they were, produced the
effect of a battalion of pretty little horses, caracol-
ing, pawing the ground, prancing, rearing and preparing to charge.   It was a charming sight; but
it all gave me no information whatever as to the
fate of Madame Cardinal.

Suddenly, I received a light tap on the shoulder.
I turned and found myself face to face with an
exceedingly pretty Polichinelle, in a great Normandy cap, with a spangled hump before and a
spangled hump behind, open-work collarette, puffed
satin shoulder-straps.   And looking out from it all
the wide-awake face of an urchin of sixteen.

"Is it you, Monsieur X——?"

"It is I."

"And are you the one that's asking about the
Cardinal family?"

"Yes, I'm the man."

"Well, if you're not afraid of going up to the
fourth tier of boxes, go and find my aunt, Madame
Canivet."

"Madame Canivet?"

"Yes. She works up on the fourth on the amphitheatre level; she'll tell you all about Madame Cardinal."

"But perhaps you know something about her yourself?"

"Mon Dieu, yes, but not much. I know well enough that ——"

But the little Polichinelle was suddenly interrupted in her tale.

"What are you doing here, Mademoiselle Canivet? Come! off with you to your place on the platform!"

It was the voice of the manager of the ballet, the affable Monsieur Pluque, who, in a black coat and white cravat, serious and dignified, superintended the evolutions of his little army corps. Mademoiselle Canivet with three leaps was in her place in the masquerade, and shouted to me again from her lofty position:

"Go and see my aunt! go and see my aunt!"

And go I did, after the ballet and during the finale. Shades of the great Mozart, forgive me! The fourth floor boxes are terribly high! I got there at last, however and hailed the first box-keeper I saw.

"Amphitheatre level?" said I.

"This is it."

"Madame Canivet?"

"That's my name."

She looked at me very closely, did Madame Canivet, and at last she cried out:

"Why, wait, I know you. You're Monsieur X——?"

"Yes, I'm Monsieur X——."

"I know you perfectly. We dined together once."

"Dined together! Where was that, pray?"

"Why, at Madame Cardinal's!"

Thereupon, in the twinkling of an eye, as if a curtain had been suddenly pulled aside, I saw the table at which Madame Canivet and I had taken our places. Yes, it was at Madame Cardinal's, at Batignolles—it must have been something like six or seven years earlier.—We had been at the Opéra one evening, at the poor old burned Opéra on Rue

Drouot. There were four of us — yes, four.; my memory was as clear as a bell. A senator, a real senator, who sat at the Luxembourg in an embroidered coat, the first secretary of a great foreign embassy, a painter, and myself, your very humble servant. It took place in a passage. There were delightful old passages in the old Opéra, with nooks and corners dimly lighted by smoky lamps. We had caught the two little Cardinals in one of the passages, and we were asking them to give us the pleasure of dining with us at the Café Anglais the next day.

The two little Cardinals were bursting to accept.

"But mamma'll never consent," they said. "You don't know mamma!"

And suddenly that redoubtable parent appeared at the end of the passage.

"Well!" she cried, "you're helping my girls to a good trouncing."

"Oh! Madame Cardinal ——"

"I don't like to have them hanging round the passages. I won't have it — I maintain it isn't proper!"

I started to push the senator forward. Madame Cardinal had great respect for the constituted authorities. The senator began:

"Come, come, Madame Cardinal, don't lose your temper; I was here and my presence ought to satisfy you. It was all innocent enough. We were simply asking the dear girls to dine with us at the Café Anglais."

"Without their mother?"

"But it would give us the greatest pleasure, Madame Cardinal, if you ——"

"The idea of the Cardinal family capering about in wine shops! Why not Monsieur Cardinal, while you're about it? Do you mean to make fun of people?"

Madame Cardinal threw this last question viciously into the senator's face; but, suddenly, she stopped, embarrassed, and changed countenance. She felt that she had gone too far. She was afraid she had offended the senator, so she undertook to set things right again.

"I beg your pardon; I was wrong, but I'm like a lioness, you know, when my daughters are in question. So you want to dine with the little ones? Well, that can be managed. Why won't you all four come and dine at the house to-morrow, without ceremony? Monsieur Cardinal will be highly honored."

We consulted one another with a glance and accepted, with the utmost seriousness, without moving a muscle, notwithstanding the inordinate desire to laugh that almost choked us.

And the next evening, having sent on ahead, in the morning, divers hampers of game and baskets of champagne, we rang Monsieur Cardinal's door-bell at half-past six.

He received us with perfect courtesy.

If we had been very critical, we might have noticed a shade of reserve in his greeting to the senator, but it was slight, very slight.

Everything went off well.

The two girls were pretty as Loves in their white muslin dresses and broad blue sashes. The father, mother and children made a delightful, almost touching picture. We seemed to be breathing an atmosphere of patriarchal virtue. We were all, beginning with Monsieur Cardinal, in black coats and white cravats. We must have looked like a nice little provincial wedding-party.

Ting-a-ling! ting-a-ling! some one rang the bell.

"That must be the *vol-au-vent!*" cries Madame Cardinal.

A little maid comes in and whispers to Madame Cardinal. Evident excitement of Madame Cardinal. She calls Virginie. A short, very animated discussion. Clearly it wasn't the vol-au-vent, but what was it? At last Virginie comes to us.

"This is what has happened," she says; "it's Madame Canivet, an old friend of mamma's, a very nice woman; she has come and invited herself to dinner. Mamma wants to send her away, but I say it wouldn't be right. Just because she's a box-keeper at the Opéra, is that any reason?"

All four of us eagerly disclaimed any such idea. We demanded Madame Canivet, our demand was acceded to. She came in. She was introduced to us, and we sat down to dinner.

What a dinner! what conversation!

I never have eaten with better appetite or more gaily. It was a little repast ordered from the cook-shop.

Madame Canivet ate heartily and drank hard, but without losing her head in the least, and whenever she could see an opening, she would carelessly inject the following phrase into the conversation, with an affable smile at the senator:

"When I think that with a little influence I might go down from the fourth tier of boxes to the third!"

The senator looked stupid, pretended not to understand, but Madame Canivet did not lose heart, and over and over again like the refrain of a ballad would come the same words:

"When I think that with a little influence," etc., etc.

At dessert, Monsieur Cardinal and the senator went at each other about the *coup d'etat.*

That capped the climax!

And now I found Madame Canivet again—still on the fourth tier—not promoted to the third. I

thought it would be polite to express astonishment thereat.

"I was going down, monsieur," she said; "I
should have gone, if it hadn't been for the 4th of
September. But let's not talk about it—I should
get too excited. What can I do for you?"

"I was told that you could give me some news
of Madame Cardinal."

"So I can, fresh news, too—up to day before
yesterday. She wrote me. But just take the
trouble to sit down."

She offered me a seat on a magnificent bench
of imitation Cordovan leather. The greatest splen-
dor reigns at the Opéra, even in the passages on
the fourth floor.

I sat down on the bench beside Madame Canivet and we settled ourselves for a little gossip.

A municipal guard in uniform was sitting at
the other end of the bench, stiff as a ramrod,
with his hands on his sabre and helmet on his
head, fast asleep. Through the little square windows of the dressing-rooms the echoes of the finale
of *Don Juan* floated softly up to our ears, and

formed an accompaniment to Madame Canivet's words.

"Madame Cardinal," she said, "has gone into the country, with Monsieur Cardinal, of course. Virginie bought a pretty little house for them at Ribeaumont, a village near Saint-Germain. She gave it to them for a wedding present. The marquis—you remember the marquis?—had the good luck to be left a widower, and married Virginie. She's a real marchioness now. I don't know what's become of Pauline, the little one. I have an idea she's gone to the bad. I've spoken to Madame Cardinal about her two or three times, and she always answers: 'I haven't got but one daughter and she's a marchioness at Florence. Don't ever say a word to me about the other.' So I don't say any more about her. You ask if Madame Cardinal enjoys herself in the country. She's bored to death there. She was used to Batignolles, you know, and when one's used to Batignolles—but she's a woman who does her duty, and as soon as she understood that Monsieur Cardinal's political future was at stake, she submitted. Bless my soul, yes, he's taken seriously to politics; he'd always dreamed of that, and in her letter of the day before yesterday Madame Cardinal says: 'Monsieur Cardinal is satisfied, very well satisfied—things are going well, very well.'"

Just then there was a great hullabaloo. All the doors were thrown open. It was the entr'acte. The curtain had fallen. Madame Canivet went off to attend to her duties, and I went down stairs.

So Monsieur Cardinal had taken seriously to politics, and was satisfied, and things were going well. It seemed to me that that phenomenon deserved to be studied close at hand.

A little trip to Ribeaumont was hardly more than a long drive, and the next day, an old cab, hired at Saint-Germain, set me down at Monsieur Cardinal's gate.

A sort of little sign was hanging on the gate, and contained this interesting notice:

Monsieur Cardinal is at the service of the electors of Ribeaumont and the neighboring Communes every day, Sundays included, from twelve o'clock till four,

*to enlighten them as to their duties and especially
as to their rights.*

*Senatorial, legislative, departmental, arrondisse-
mental, municipal and other elections.*

That was a good beginning. I rang. The next
moment I heard a voice, a well-known voice:
"Amélie! Amélie! The bell, the bell!" I heard
footsteps coming hurriedly along the path, and
found myself confronted by a little maid.

"Have you come about politics? Are you an
elector?"

"No, no—I would like to speak to Madame
Cardinal ——"

I was interrupted by an outcry. Madame
Cardinal had recognized me, and she ran — at
least she did the best she could in the way of
running. Her scanty locks floated mildly in the
wind, her spectacles jumped up and down on her
nose, her broad face was made still broader by
enthusiasm, and these words came from her pant-
ing breast:

"You! you! it's you!"

Never before, I think, had I been welcomed with such demonstrations of joy and affection. I was a little ashamed.

Monsieur Cardinal was more dignified. He received me at the top of the steps, led me through his reception-room, opened a door, and said, with a majestic wave of the hand:

"Enter — enter the salon — I might say the temple."

I looked at him in some amazement and repeated:

"The temple?"

"Yes. Look. My God! That is my God! There on the mantelpiece."

I tried to see, but the temple was dark. I could distinguish a dark object on the chimney-piece, but I could hardly make out ——

"Voltaire! it's Voltaire! Do you know that bust of Voltaire?"

Did I know that bust of Voltaire! Why, I bought it myself! My friend Paul was in England, and one morning I received a letter from him.

"Pray read this letter of Virginie's," he wrote me, "and do what is necessary."

This is what Virginie's letter said almost word for word:

" My Dear Friend:

'Papa's birthday comes next week. We used to celebrate Saint-Michel's day, but he won't let us now; he says that celebrating saints' days is giving countenance to superstition. So we celebrate his birthday. It comes to the same thing about presents. You know how sensitive papa is, and how proud! He never asks for anything directly, but he always finds some clever way of letting me know what he would like, without seeming to do it. For the last two weeks, he's been talking about a bust of Voltaire from morning till night, at breakfast and dinner, all the time in fact.— 'Oh! if I only had a bust of Voltaire! I saw a fine one, in bronze, life size, on Boulevard Poissonière,' etc., etc. Voltaire's his God, you know! So it would be very nice of you to write from over there to one of your friends to buy the bust and send it to our house. Don't let him make any mistake. It's a bust with the head bent forward, and a smile on the face. Papa says it's just Voltaire's smile. But don't let the dealer make a fool of himself, like the one last year about the piece of furniture for the parlor. You know they

sent a card and a receipted bill in your name with it.
Papa kept it all the same, but he was in a sort of dumb
rage for a fortnight. He wouldn't speak to mamma or
me. Let them just send the bust without a card or a
bill.''

So there we three were, Monsieur Cardinal,
Madame Cardinal and I, sitting around the fire-
place under the presidency of Voltaire.

We began to talk, but our talk did not answer
my purpose at all. It was hardly more than a
monologue by Monsieur Cardinal. He proposed
to serve his country to the full extent of his
powers. Paris was too vast a stage for him, that
fact he recognized. But he had already rendered
great services to Ribeaumont, and proposed to
render greater still. He had to deal with very
narrow minds, far behind the age. Worthy people,
but poor, and wholly absorbed in their fields and
vineyards. He would rouse them out of their
apathy. He, the bold pioneer of universal suffrage,
would go to the root of matters, etc., etc.

He droned on—and on. This sort of thing had
lasted a quarter of an hour, and I was beginning

Chapter Three

THE LITTLE CARDINALS

———

Suddenly, I received a light tap on the shoulder. I turned and found myself face to face with an exceedingly pretty Polichinelle, in a great Normandy cap, with a spangled hump before and a spangled hump behind, open-work collarette, puffed satin shoulder-straps. And looking out from it all the wide-awake face of an urchin of sixteen.

to regret my expedition to Ribeaumont. What I must have was a little chat, tête-à-téte, with Madame Cardinal.

Luckily, in the middle of one of Monsieur Cardinal's harangues, the bell rang.

Monsieur Cardinal raised his head and pricked up his ears. His face lighted up. He smelt powder.

Suppose it should be an elector? It was one!

The little maid showed him into the salon.

He was an atrocious creature, was the elector. Boots trodden down at the heel, threadbare blouse, soft hat, cravat like a string, waxed moustaches. Abominable, in short; abominable!

Monsieur Cardinal darted to meet him.

"You wish to speak to me, my friend?"

"Yes, on the subject of my registration. Just fancy—they propose to strike off my name because of a paltry judgment for four sous."

"Come, my friend, come into my study."

And Monsieur Cardinal entered his study, having most respectfully waved his precious client in before him.

I was alone with Madame Cardinal. I had no need to touch the spring to set the machinery in motion. The words gushed out of themselves, abundant and artless, from Madame Cardinal's lips.

"How glad I am to see you! Ah! you remind me of old times—the good old times—the Opéra, Madame Monge's box; Madame Dominique's lesson. And it's all over now. We had to banish ourselves to the country. I have sacrificed myself, my dear sir, positively sacrificed myself. You know what took place under the Commune. Monsieur Cardinal accepted a place in the magistracy; he was arrested; they were going to send him to the hulks; the marquis saw Monsieur Thiers; Monsieur Cardinal was restored to us. But people began to wonder in Batignolles how Monsieur Cardinal went to work to recover his liberty. And they got at the truth of it. His daughter a marquis's mistress! And that marquis, a friend of Monsieur Thiers! It was all up with Monsieur Cardinal in Batignolles. The pure creatures began to turn their backs on him and heap insults on insults. That didn't shake Monsieur Cardinal's convictions, but it saddened him. That was when he began to talk about going to live in the country. There were useful truths to be spread among the rural population. And to spread truths has always been Monsieur Cardinal's passion! 'There's something of the apostle in me,' he often says to me, 'I feel the need of spreading truth.' However, I don't need to say any more about that. You know Monsieur Cardinal's character."

"I know it, Madame Cardinal, I know it perfectly."

"And then there was another thing: there was the state of siege in Paris. Monsieur Cardinal was near dying of that state of siege; he did nothing but repeat:

"'I'm stifling, I'm stifling under this state of siege. I feel as if I had a weight here. I don't know how you go to work to breathe; I can't— I cannot!'

"And every evening, when it was time for the patrol to pass, he had a horrible spasm. You know, during the time immediately following the

Commune, mounted patrols rode through all the streets.

"At Batignolles they were cuirassiers. At quarter to nine every evening, regularly, they passed under our windows.

"From eight to half-past eight Monsieur Cardinal began to grow excited. He seemed to smell the patrol coming.

"I'd say to him:

"'My dear, if it troubles you so much to see them pass, don't stay here, go to your little café.'

"'No, no,' he'd say. 'I might meet them, and I don't know what would happen! No, I don't know! and then, too, it's all for the best, for it keeps my wrath alive, it keeps it alive!'

"So he stayed at home. And when the horses' hoofs clattered under our windows Monsieur Cardinal would turn livid. He wouldn't say a word. It was awful to see him.

"Sometimes he'd drag himself to the window, and say:

"'Bare sabres! their sabres are bare!'

"In the midst of all his trouble, the poor man was going to seed. I got along all right, so far as I was concerned; I had the Opéra and I had Pauline."

"Ah! yes, Pauline — pray, tell me something about Pauline."

"Yes, I will tell you about her, but nobody else. There's a sore spot in our family, and that sore spot is Pauline.

"She disturbed me, Pauline did.

"In the first place, she didn't work at her dancing, and when a child doesn't work at her dancing it's bad—it's a sign she has ideas in her head. And then, you know, that wasn't Virginie's nature at all. Virginie was so confiding, so affectionate, so entirely as she ought to be with her mother— always consulting me about everything. Pauline on the other hand avoided me, got away from me. She wasn't so open and unreserved about her future and her hopes as a child ought to be with her mother.

"I kept close watch; but when a girl's determined to go to the devil the most watchful mother

that ever was can't do anything, you know.   I
used to see a young fellow always hanging and
hanging about Pauline in the wings.   I had questioned her about him and she said:

"'He's a nice sort of a fellow, and he's in a good
position—secretary to a minister.'

"Secretary to a minister!   What sort of a position's that in a country where ministers fall like
card-houses?

"At last, one day, lo and behold Pauline makes
a clean breast to me, tells me that she loves this
ne'er-do-well, that she adores him, that she's dying
for him, that she wants to give herself to him for
love!   Did ever you hear such nonsense?   Not
to mention another thing.   Pauline knew Monsieur
Cardinal's political opinions.

"However, her father would have forgiven
everything—yes, anything—except a public functionary of Monsieur MacMahon's government!   I
gave Pauline a good talking to, and I gave her
to understand that I wouldn't have her talking to
her jumping-jack of a minister's secretary any
more.   She pretended to be convinced by my

arguments. And, that very evening—do you know what happened that evening, my dear monsieur—do you know?"

"I suspect, Madame Cardinal."

"That evening—they were playing *Robert*—she slipped through my fingers after the ballet of the Nuns. Everybody came down—no Pauline! I didn't know where the jumping-jack lived. If I had, I'd have gone there at breakneck speed to take back my child. But there, I couldn't go to all the departments and ring and ask the concierge:

"'Does it happen to be your minister's secretary —— ?'

"I went home: Monsieur Cardinal turned pale when he saw me alone.

"I fell on my knees.

"'Forgive me, Monsieur Cardinal, forgive me. I have been a bad mother; I haven't been watchful enough.'

"He picked me up and kissed me and we wept together. He's admirable at such times, is Monsieur Cardinal!

"She came back the next day, the little wretch, and we were weak enough to forgive her. But when a child has played a trick like that on you, you see, you can't have any more confidence in her. Monsieur Cardinal used to say to me, sadly enough :

"'You see, Madame Cardinal, she's a child that will get away from us; she won't cheer our old age. She won't be like Virginie!'

"Ah! Virginie! what an angel! I'll tell you about her in a minute when I'm done with Pauline, and that won't be long.

"She left the ballet, did Pauline, she has a house and horses and carriages, but she's forgotten her family! I only asked one favor of her. I said to her:

"'Look here, your father has a political future ahead of him, so don't, I beg of you, drag the name of Cardinal in the mud. Change your name.'

"'That's been done a month, mamma,' says she. 'Pauline Cardinal—There wasn't any style about that. My name's Pauline de Giraldas.'"

"Is she Madame de Giraldas?"

" Yes, that's her—and the Marquise Cavalcanti is my angel, my Virginie! He married her, my dear monsieur, he married her! She lives in a Palace at Florence—and she lives up to her rank—and she's received everywhere—and she makes people respect her—and no lovers! Monsieur Cardinal and I went to Florence to see her. We passed a week in her palace. The marquis was as nice as could be. He loaded us down with presents.

" 'It's a pleasure to receive presents that you can receive without hanging your head,' said Monsieur Cardinal—'presents from a real son-in-law. And then, in spite of the political chasm that separates us, I must admit that the man has good blood, that he knows how to give, and gives nobly.'

" We meant to come back to Paris at once, but just at the last minute Monsieur Cardinal changed his mind.

" ' Madame Cardinal,' he says, ' suppose we push on to Rome?'

" ' To Rome, Monsieur Cardinal! look out, that's the land of priests. Do you think you can see such a place without getting excited?'

"'Yes, Madame Cardinal, I long to see that den of superstition.'

"And we went to Rome.

"All the way Monsieur Cardinal kept saying to me:

"'I am perfectly sure, Madame Cardinal, that Rome will leave me quite cool.'

"And, indeed, it did leave him cool. We saw all there was to see except the inside of the churches, because Monsieur Cardinal wouldn't put his foot inside them; and everywhere Monsieur Cardinal said just the same thing:

"'It's overdone, Madame Cardinal, it's overdone!'

"Rome with all its churches and convents exasperated him.

"'It's a dead city, Madame Cardinal,' said he, 'a city that ought to be wiped off the face of the earth. Look you—I don't know anything about Chicago, but I prefer Chicago. It's alive, at least, is Chicago!'

"After three days, Monsieur Cardinal had enough of it. It made him ill to breathe the air. It gave him spasms and dyspepsia. So we were about packing our trunks when a waiter at the hotel took us aside and said:

"'His Holiness gives an audience to-day at four o'clock and I've got two tickets, would you like 'em ?'

"'My friend,' says I, 'if you knew Monsieur Cardinal better, you wouldn't make such a suggestion.'

"But Monsieur Cardinal interrupted me.

"'Excuse me, Madame Cardinal, excuse me. I wouldn't have sought this meeting, but as the opportunity offers itself we'll go to the Vatican.'

"And we went. I wasn't sorry to see the thing myself, but my uneasiness was about Monsieur Cardinal. He promised me he'd be calm and hold himself back, but I knew the violence of his character and I knew the pope was his *bête noire*.

"We arrived and were shown into a lovely room, and someone told us we must kneel when His Holiness was announced.—Monsieur Cardinal, kneel!—I says to myself:

" ' Whatever will happen? Monsieur Cardinal will never consent to kneel before a mortal man.'

" The door opened—they announced His Holiness. Monsieur Cardinal got down on his knees. To tell you the truth I didn't know what to make of it. And the pope approached us.

" Ah! my word! at that moment what could you expect? I had a little religion in my childhood, and I should have it still if it wasn't for Monsieur Cardinal—and then I'm not strong—I'm a woman. In short I was upset with emotion. I had tears in my eyes. It seemed to me as if I was taking my first communion over again.

" But lo and behold, all of a sudden, just when the pope was square in front of us, up jumps Monsieur Cardinal, never bows at all, but stares proudly at the pope, right in the eye, man to man —— "

At that moment the door of Monsieur Cardinal's study opened. It was the elector. He had put on his soft hat. He had taken an old rubber tobacco-pouch from his pocket and was filling his pipe. A vague odor of tobacco and alcohol floated about his person.

Monsieur Cardinal showed him to the door with the utmost respect, and said, bowing deferentially:

" At your service, my friend, always at your service!"

IV

MADAME CANIVET

IV

MADAME CANIVET

Five years later, once more at the Opéra, Friday, May 28, 1880, about ten o'clock in the evening— we must be precise when we are dealing with matters of such importance—I had gone to have a chat with my old friend Madame X——, between the

IV

MADAME CANIVET

Five years later, once more at the Opéra, Friday, May 28, 1880, about ten o'clock in the evening— we must be precise when we are dealing with matters of such importance—I had gone to have a chat with my old friend Madame X——, between the

97

second and third acts of *Aïda*. Before I entered her
box I handed my coat to the box-keeper, but without noticing that obliging functionary's countenance.

My visit at an end I left the box, and lo! the
good woman said to me, as she helped me on with
my coat:

"Monsieur has been very well since the little
visit he paid me three or four years ago?"

"Visit! What visit?"

"Oh, yes! up yonder. I was box-keeper on the
fourth tier, and you came and asked me about the
Cardinal family. I'm Madame Canivet."

Madame Canivet! I remembered instantly. It
was Madame Canivet who put me on the track of
the Cardinal family the night of the reproduction
of *Don Juan*.

To go down to the third tier was the extent of
Madame Canivet's ambition at that time. That
ambition had been more than satisfied. I found
Madame Canivet now on the first tier.

I congratulated her on that fact.

"Ah! yes," she replied, "this is how it happened.
I am concierge in the Quarter de la Madeleine. Well,

there's been such a quantity of changes of ministers these last days that I finally got one—a minister, I mean,—in my house. He spoke to the manager of the Opéra and I came down to the first tier."

I congratulated Madame Canivet anew and took advantage of the opportunity to ask for news of Madame Cardinal.

"Madame Cardinal—Oh! she's well, the dear woman. Still in the country with her husband. But very sad, all broken up, because—just fancy ; you wouldn't believe it—Monsieur Cardinal hasn't got a place in the government yet."

"No place?"

"Not the smallest. She wrote me last week, and she says poor Monsieur Cardinal is completely discouraged, so much so that he's talking about giving up politics."

"Oho! and does Madame Cardinal write you often ?"

"Very often."

"And you keep her letters ?"

"Piously, monsieur, piously. They're so interesting, so touching! She's a fine woman, Madame

Cardinal, a woman who never knew but two things: her husband and her duty."

"I know, I know. I've always been very fond of Madame Cardinal."

"So has she of you. Why, in last week's letter, she said: 'Now you've come down to the first tier, you ought to see some of those gentlemen very often. Give them my regards.' And your name was among them, monsieur—the very first."

"I am touched, deeply touched, and I would like very much to read that letter."

"That and the others, too, if it will gratify you. I'll bring them to you day after to-morrow."

And so, two days later, I had the honor of receiving thirty or forty letters from Madame Cardinal from the hands of Madame Canivet. Don't be alarmed. I have no intention of publishing Madame Cardinal's correspondence entire. Four letters will suffice. Those four I will reproduce faithfully, *verbatim et literatim*, without adding or subtracting a single word. I have simply corrected the mistakes in orthography. At first I thought of letting them stand, but there were too many.

These letters chronicle the history of the Cardinal family during the last four years, and at the same time, incidentally, a little of the history of all of us.

V

MONSIEUR CARDINAL'S PLATFORM

V

MONSIEUR CARDINAL'S PLATFORM

"RIBEAUMONT, November 25, 1877.

"You ask me for news of us all, my dear friend. The news is good, and not good. So far as regards health, we're all well; Virginie in Florence, Pauline in Paris, Monsieur Cardinal and

V

MONSIEUR CARDINAL'S PLATFORM

RIXEAUMONT, November 25, 1874.

You ask me for news of us all, my dear friend. The news is good and not good. So far as regards health, we're all well: Virginie in Florence, Pauline in Paris, Monsieur Cardinal and

Ch Léandre inv.   L. Muller sc.

V

MONSIEUR CARDINAL'S PLATFORM

"RIBEAUMONT, November 25, 1877.

"You ask me for news of us all, my dear friend. The news is good, and not good. So far as regards health, we're all well; Virginie in Florence, Pauline in Paris, Monsieur Cardinal and

I here in the country. But alas! we're all well, each on her own hook. No more family joys. No more home life.

"Oh dear! it's very hard to have been all your life a woman devoted to home and duty; never to have loved but one thing in the world, your own fireside; to feel that you are, at the same time, a wife and a mother; to say to yourself: 'I have two girls and those girls aren't here and never will be here to comfort my old age.'

"Virginie, married to the marquis, Virginie, a marchioness for good and all, continues to be the ornament of the first Italian society in Florence.

"Ah! poor chick, all her grandeur don't turn her head. Only last week she wrote me that she was the queen of all the fêtes and pleasure parties down there, but that it didn't amount to anything, that there was no fun in being a marchioness at Florence every day, and that she often longed for her family, and Batignolles and the Opéra.

"She's an angel! she allows us six thousand francs a year.

"She often talks of coming to France to see us; but, although my mother-heart bleeds for her, I have the courage to discourage it. I wouldn't dare to bring the marquis and Monsieur Cardinal together again. You know there was always a political chasm between them, but, in spite of that, they had a certain amount of respect for each other. They insulted each other, but esteemed each other all the time. Aside from politics, their relations were cordial, almost affectionate.

"Alas! there haven't been any relations at all between them since what happened at Rome in 1875 between the pope and Monsieur Cardinal.

"I've told you about that. In an audience at the Vatican, Monsieur Cardinal refused to bow to the pope and looked him square in the face, in the eyes without winking.

"They found out at the court of Rome that Monsieur Cardinal was the marquis's father-in-law; they wrote to the marquis from Rome, and the marquis wrote Monsieur Cardinal a high and mighty letter from Florence; Monsieur Cardinal replied with a high and mightier one still, and all relations were broken off, except—of course—the pension of six thousand francs, which was provided for in Virginie's contract anyway.

"As to Pauline, she began to go wrong, and she's kept on. She's now the swellest kind of a great *cocotte* under the name of Madame de Giraldas,— and very often, when Monsieur Cardinal's reading his newspaper, I see a frown on his face. Then I know that it's—I know there's something about Madame de Giraldas's fine house or her dresses or her carriages.

"Pauline is rich, Pauline is happy, Pauline don't need her mother,—or rather she thinks she don't need her mother. She makes a mistake— a girl always needs her mother, especially in her position.

"I've been to see her two or three times on the sly, at her house on Rue Kepler.

"Ah! such *chic*, my dear, such *chic!* And, from one point of view, it's almost flattering for a mother to see her child living in such *chic*.

"She has eleven servants!—yes, eleven :—day coachman, night coachman, first lady's maid, second lady's maid, major-domo, chief cook, scullery-wench, footman, grooms and a tiger. And all so well set-up and so well trained, and not familiar. Real great folks' servants.

" But think how much it all costs!

" You ought to see how she's pillaged and robbed by all those people. I ran my eye over the cook's book, and I tell you, knowing the price of things as I do, it made me shudder.

"So much so that I tried to make Monsieur Cardinal listen to reason.

"I said to him one day:

"'Listen to me, Monsieur Cardinal—there's horrible pilfering going on at Pauline's. Let me go to Paris once a week. It's a mother's duty to keep an eye on her child, to prevent her being eaten out of house and home.'

" At that Monsieur Cardinal turned white as a sheet; he got up and, without saying a word, went coldly and opened the door. He makes me tremble at such times. He's so solemn and theatrical! After opening the door he stepped back a little way and said with a dramatic gesture:

"'You may go, Madame Cardinal, but adieu—adieu forever!'

"At that, as you can imagine, I flopped down on a sofa with my heels in the air, in convulsions.

"Abandon Monsieur Cardinal! Abandon him at this moment when he's just girding his loins, as he says, for his great battle, when he's beginning what he calls his rural apostolate, when he's wearing himself out, body and soul, for justice and truth ——

"Abandon him, never!

"Ah! my, dear, he has a hard time, I tell you, in his apostolate. He finds the peasants sluggish, not enough interested in politics. He wants to spread the agitation in the country districts, but that's not an easy thing to do, for, except an old lady who's a Legitimist, an old gentleman who's an Orléanist and four or five former office-holders who are Bonapartists, everybody round here is for the Republic. But they're republicans in their own way. Country republicans aren't the same thing at all as the republicans of Batignolles. They're all people who think that things haven't gone badly these last four or five years, that the wheat keeps on growing and the grapes ripening, that prices keep well up at the Market, that they're left in peace, that they'd better be content with that, and that when you have any sort of a government you'd better hang on to it as long as you can.

"No later than yesterday an old vine-dresser said to Monsieur Cardinal, who jumped into the air at every word:

"'For my part I'd have liked to see Charles X. stay on, I'd have liked to see Louis-Philippe stay on, I'd have liked to see Napoléon stay on, and now I'd like to see the Republic stay on. I've always been for the government that's in. I wouldn't have voted to have the Republic, but now we have it, I vote to keep it. That's my opinion. I've always been for keeping what we've got.'

"Such opinions as that put Monsieur Cardinal in such a state!

"Monsieur Cardinal has always been for progress. He says France ought never to stand still, that she ought to keep going forward, forward. He says she's the advance guard of the nations, the pioneer of civilization.

"All this, you understand, my dear friend, is Monsieur Cardinal's statements and expressions; but, by hearing him say them over and over again, I almost know them by heart. He's worked hard since we came into the country; he's begun to read the Latin authors—in French, of course. He's made great progress in literature and politics and eloquence.

"Yesterday he said to me:

"'Madame Cardinal, I feel that I am ripe for power!'

"If he says so, it must be so, for a modester man don't breathe. If you knew how well he speaks now—and how long! Such fine things as he says to me in private, and it's all lost to the country; nobody hears it all but me, and three-quarters of the time I don't understand a word of it.

"What I can't understand is, why they don't come to Monsieur Cardinal and say to him:

"'Take your choice—what place would you like? in the treasury or the magistracy?'

Chapter Five

MONSIEUR CARDINAL'S PLATFORM

"*Monsieur Cardinal commenced a parley with the peasant.*

* * * * * * * * * *

"'*So you're turning up your field.*'

"'*As you see.*'

"'*And if your field wasn't turned up, what would happen?*'

"'*Bless me! it would happen that it wouldn't yield anything.*'

"'*That's what I expected you would answer me. The country's precisely like your field; it must of necessity be turned up, it must be constantly turned up.*'"

"Those are the two things that would suit him best.

"We have the Republic and Monsieur Cardinal with nothing to do!

"Why, what kind of a thing is this Republic that might make use of Monsieur Cardinal and don't make use of him?

"Here he is devouring himself, consuming himself, pining away, ready to accept any office whatsoever, even a well-paid one.

"From morning till night, Monsieur Cardinal thinks of nothing but his country, and from night till morning too, for very often he wakes up in the night to think about it. All of a sudden I'll hear a voice in the darkness, saying:

"'Light up, Madame Cardinal, light up!'

"You see, some idea about reform or progress has come into his head. He's afraid that it'll escape him, so he wants to write it down at once. As I'm on the side where the matches are, I light up. I pass him his little note-book and his little pencil, and there he writes away in the middle of the night for his country.

" Why, last night I lighted the candle three times
for three different thoughts that came into Monsieur
Cardinal's mind.   The first was about the apathy of
the country districts ; the second about Voltaire; the
third about a religion entirely without priests. When
the matches wouldn't light, Monsieur Cardinal flew
into a rage and shouted :

" ' They do it on purpose, those fellows of the
Left Centre, the Orléanists in the government, to
bring discredit on the Republic ! To think that
matches aren't as good under the Republic as they
were under the Empire ! '

" This match question is a very important one
in the country.   A Bonapartist in a neighboring
village said to Monsieur Cardinal yesterday, sar-
castically :

" ' Your Republic doesn't even know how to make
matches.'

" ' They're not my Republic's matches', says Monsieur Cardinal, ' they're Monsieur de MacMahon's.'

" He's forever making retorts like that; they
come into his head like a flash, without his hunting
for them or thinking about them.

"As I told you, it upsets me to have them not employ Monsieur Cardinal. But it don't seem to astonish him.

"'If they don't come to me, Madame Cardinal,' he says to me yesterday, 'it's because the present Republic isn't the true Republic. The true Republic is progress, uproar, fever.'

"Monsieur Cardinal has studied history a great deal lately; he says history's a mine and it's astonishing how much one finds in it. He's discovered that there used to be republics long ago, and that those republics were always in an uproar; that people lived out of doors, in the streets and public squares; that there was constant excitement in the—in the—the —— He used a devil of a Latin word that I can't remember. I'll go and ask him what it was. He's going to spell it for me.—*F-o—Fo—r-u-m—rum.*—It isn't spelt the same but it's pronounced like *rhum* (rum) the liquor.

"He tells all this to the people hereabouts, Monsieur Cardinal does, and you ought to hear him talk to the peasants. It's fine, I tell you.

"Every day, from twelve o'clock till four, no matter what the weather is, rain or shine, he travels about the country. He stops and talks with the peasants, but he don't use his usual language with them—that would be too much, for them, they wouldn't understand it—so he makes himself small, he goes down to their level.

"Last Tuesday he took me with him. We stopped by a peasant who was digging up his field. Monsieur Cardinal commenced a parley with the peasant.

"'Well, my friend.'

"'Well, Monsieur Cardinal.'

"'So you're turning up your field.'

"'As you see.'

"'And if your field wasn't turned up, what would happen?'

"'Bless me! it would happen that it wouldn't yield anything.'

"'That's what I expected you would answer me. The country's precisely like your field; it must of necessity be turned up, it must be constantly turned up.'

" 'Oh! no, it ain't the same thing ; my field needs to be turned up, but the country needs to be let alone.'

" There's your peasant! They always stick to the same old path.

" But Monsieur Cardinal isn't discouraged. He says that he'll end by stirring up Seine-et-Oise. Meantime he's stirring me up!

" All this politics is dancing round in my head. I'm beginning to think I understand something about it. I read the political newspapers now,—I, who used to read nothing but the novels and crimes and accidents in my *Petit Journal,* as you know.

" There's something else that Monsieur Cardinal's all worked up about—that's the centenary of Voltaire. It isn't till May 30th, next year, but he's getting ready for it now.

" He'd like to give a lecture here at Ribeaumont. The title of his lecture will be *Voltaire the God.* Monsieur Cardinal knows his whole lecture by heart already; and you ought to see how he'll spout it at you.

"Now and then in the evening, after dinner, he repeats his lecture to me. I sit down in front of him. I represent the audience. Monsieur Cardinal takes his head in his hands. He pretends to be collecting his thoughts, to be thinking up his first sentence. He isn't really thinking it up, because he knows it all by heart, but he looks as if he was.

"All of a sudden he raises his head, pushes back his hair with a little quick movement of his right hand, and begins:

"'A frivolous, although profound writer has called Voltaire *King Voltaire*. The word *king* is an insult. I will not throw it in Voltaire's face. I will call him *Voltaire the God*, apologizing for the use of the expression because of the superstitious veneration attaching to it; but it's one way of purifying it, to apply it to Voltaire.'

"And he goes on with a long harangue about Voltaire as a republican.

"That must last an hour and he pretends to be making it up all the time. The lecture's all written, and who do you suppose wrote it?

"I did, my dear friend, I did! Monsieur Cardinal thought best to give me a share in his labors.

"He dictated it to me. For some time now he's been practising dictating, even to several people at once.

"So, last Sunday, he sent for the mayor's secretary and the schoolmaster. He seated those two men at three tables, and began to dictate to all three of us—at the same time—three different things. To the mayor's secretary, a note against tyranny; to the schoolmaster, reflections on the crimes of popes; to me a memorandum about an army entirely made up of civilians.

"He got a little mixed up, to be sure, here and there—but only a very little. He walked up and down and sweated great drops. I really pitied him.

"'You'll kill yourself, Monsieur Cardinal,' I says to him; 'it's too much work.'

"'I must do it—I must do it!' he answered.

"And next Sunday he's going to begin again. All this frightens me. I wonder how a single human brain can hold so many things.

"Every night, after dinner, he dictates his impressions, his recollections—the journal of his life. It'll be very interesting, but it can't be published till fifty years after his death, when, as he says, passions will have died out.

"Monsieur Cardinal is also preparing his platform for the elections to the Municipal Council. He won't enter political life till then.

"He don't want to go too fast. The Municipal Council first—then the Council General—and then, no one knows—no one knows.

"Monsieur Cardinal says to me only last night:

"'You see, Madame Cardinal, with universal suffrage anything is possible!'

"This platform of Monsieur Cardinal's will be a platform that means something!—it will be the platform he'll stand on all his life. It seems there are politicians who issue addresses, and then, when they're once where they want to be, why it's 'go to the devil with my platform!' Monsieur Cardinal don't feed on that kind of bread.

"Drawing up his platform caused a touching scene between us. The other evening he says to me:

"'Well,' he says, 'I've decided on my platform. Sit down, Madame Cardinal, and I'll dictate to you.'

"So I sits down, and he begins. Freedom of this, freedom of that. There were twenty lines for all the freedoms and then, at the end, the whole thing in a nutshell: 'freedom of everything.'

"'Re-establishment of divorce,' Monsieur Cardinal goes on.

"At that, my dear, I jumps up from my chair, I looks Monsieur Cardinal square in the eye, bold as a lion, and I says:

"'I won't write that, Monsieur Cardinal, I won't write that, and if you care anything for me, you'll strike that horror out of your programme. When a man's married a woman like me and had the luck to marry one of his daughters to a marquis that's a millionaire three times over, he shouldn't have such ideas. You're my admiration, my religion, I worship you like a God, but my hand shall drop off before I write such an atrocious thing.'

"Then he comes to me and takes my two hands.

"'Look you, Madame Cardinal,' he says, 'I'm going to make a great sacrifice to please you; I never bargained with my principles as you know. Well, for your sake, I abandon divorce, I strike it out of my platform. But let's not waste time— let's go on, let's go on.'

"He tried to go on with his dictation, but I couldn't—my sobs were choking me. I was taken with a spasm of weeping. He sacrificed divorce to me!

"I fell at his feet and kissed his hands. Haven't I reason to adore that man?

"I got over it at last. We went on with the platform. I wrote down whatever he wanted me to —*Expulsion of the Jesuits—Suppression of all forms of worship*, etc., etc.

"I might have had a few little remarks to make on that subject. You know I've always kept a little bit of religious feeling. I think that superior men, like Monsieur Cardinal, can get along without any sort of religion. But there are only a small number of such men—they're the exception, the chosen few; and it seems to me that for the others, the bulk of the common people, it would be a good thing to have the fear or the hope of something else after this short life.

"I deserve some credit for talking like that, for I had good reason to complain of religion once, my word! It was a long time ago, under the empire, the day before Virginie was to come out of the crowd at last. It was a reproduction of *Guillaume Tell;* Virginie was to dance for the first time in a *pas de quatre;* indeed she had a little bit of work to do all by herself, with pirouetting and tiptoeing both; that made me uneasy, for Virginie was better on her toes than she was in keeping her skirts filled out.

"I had already burnt a dozen tapers in a dozen different churches. Tapers are the things. Nobody asks you who they're for, or what. You give two sous, five sous, according to the size, they light your taper and it burns for whatever you choose. But the night before the performance, I says to myself:

"'Tapers ain't enough for a début at the Opéra. I must have a mass.'

"So off I goes to Sainte-Marie des Batignolles. I found a little vicar there who seemed in a great hurry. I says to him:

"'Monsieur l'Abbé, this is for a mass.'

"'For when?'

"'For to-morrow.'

"'For a dead person?'

"'What! for a dead person—not at all; it's for my oldest daughter, who isn't dead by any means, because she makes her début at the Opéra to-morrow, and that's just why I want a mass said.'

"'A mass for a début at the Opéra!'

"And with that my little vicar swells up and turns his back on me, saying that there ain't any masses for that sort of thing. No masses for that sort of thing, indeed!

"And why not, I'd like to know? Was it my fault, that I was born in humble circumstances and my daughter was in the ballet instead of in the aristocracy? Any way, she's in the aristocracy now!

"She don't need their nasty little Batignolles masses any more. She has her priedieu now, in red velvet, with her crest, in the flushest church in Florence.

"Write to me and tell me the news at the Opéra.

"Your affectionate friend,

"ZOÉ CARDINAL."

VI

PAULINE CARDINAL

VI

PAULINE CARDINAL

"RIBEAUMONT, May 12, 1878.

"Oh! my dear friend, such a week! Such joy at first and then such sorrow! Sunday was the election for the Municipal Council. Monsieur Cardinal was a candidate. He was elected! You can't form any idea of Monsieur Cardinal's delight.

VI

PAULINE CARDINAL

"RIBEAUMONT, May 12, 1878.

"Oh! my dear friend, such a week! Such joy at
first and then such sorrow! Sunday was the election for the Municipal Council. Monsieur Cardinal
was a candidate. He was elected! You can't form
any idea of Monsieur Cardinal's delight.

"' *I am something! At last, I am something!
this is the first step!*'

"He did nothing but repeat that. He couldn't
sit still. He went in and out, and walked all round
the house.

"He wanted me to go and see the hall where
the Council meets, to show me where his seat
would be. That evening he couldn't eat any dinner; that night he couldn't sleep.

"Two or three times he just dozed off, and then
he'd wake up with a jump and begin again:

"' *I am something at last! This is the first
step!*'

"I was awfully put about to see him in such a
state of excitement. I tried to calm him down. I
made him some drink in the middle of the night—
limes and poppy-tops.

"' You must sleep, Monsieur Cardinal,' I told
him; 'you must sleep or else you won't have any
strength for the struggle that's coming.'

"For there is a struggle coming, my dear friend.
Monsieur Cardinal won't be elected mayor, and he
expects to be. The old mayor is going to have a

majority again in the Council. He's a great manufacturer, retired from business—very rich—two or
three millions. He's one of those men who, according to Monsieur Cardinal, make a bad use of their
money by scattering it round through the province
without discrimination, giving to everybody in every
direction, for schools and churches, libraries and
hospitals. That isn't charity, it's ostentation.

" Monsieur Cardinal can't meet him on that
ground. He hasn't got money by the shovelful.
He has just a modest, honorable competence. He
could afford to give a little something now and then,
but he never gives anything. It's a matter of
principle with him. He'd blush to succeed by such
means. He wants to owe everything to his personal
worth.

" Monsieur Cardinal has decided to take up the
cudgels with the mayor right away. He's preparing an address for the first sitting.

" But don't make any mistake. It will be a political address without seeming to be, because there's
a stupid law that municipal councils sha'n't meddle
with anything but the affairs of the Commune. But

it would be a great pity if Monsieur Cardinal didn't know how to get around the law after all he's studied. It seems that getting around the law is the A, B, C of politics.

"Five days after the election, that is to say, day before yesterday, Friday, was Monsieur Cardinal's birthday.

"Wednesday morning I had a very pretty, sweet little note from Pauline:

"'Dear mamma, it troubles you to have me at variance with papa, and I don't like it either. Friday will be papa's birthday. If I dared, I'd come and dine with you in the country. I could leave my carriage at Pavillon Henri IV. and take a cab from Saint-Germain so as not to shock papa. Tell me if I may chance it.

"'Of course I should bring a present for papa.

"'Write me and tell me what he'd like,' etc., etc.

"The postman always hands me Pauline's letters on the sly, and I read them on the sly, at the foot of the garden.

"All of a sudden, while I was reading this one over and over, I saw Monsieur Cardinal coming.

There was such loving, wheedling words for me at the end of the letter, that I was all upset. I felt my eyes full of tears just asking leave to flow.

"'Is that a letter from Pauline?' Monsieur Cardinal asked me, sternly.

"'Yes.'

"'More scandal!'

"That was unjust. My tears overflowed, and I sobbed as I handed the letter to Monsieur Cardinal.

"'Here,' I said, 'read it.'

"He took the letter, and after he'd read it, he said:

"'I was wrong, Madame Cardinal, I was wrong; this idea of giving me a present.—The poor child still has some right feeling. Come, as I've just had a great joy, I want you to have one too. I don't want to know how Pauline lives—whether she has a fine house and horses and diamonds——'

"'Does she have them!!!'

"That was a foolish thing for me to say. It was an outburst of maternal pride.

"'I don't want to know,' Monsieur Cardinal continued. 'Between now and to-morrow I'll think up some way that Pauline can come here on my birthday. I'll think it over to-night. I get to the bottom of things when I'm lying awake at night.'

"Sure enough, about two o'clock in the morning, Monsieur Cardinal shook me and said:

"'I've thought out how it can be done. If she chooses, Pauline can pass some time with us—a week or ten days.'

"'A week or ten days!'

"'Yes. But let her come very simply dressed. We'll say she's a niece of ours—a shop-girl in Paris —that she isn't very well, and we're taking her in for charity. That will have a good effect. You can go to-morrow morning and fetch Pauline.'

"At eleven o'clock the next day I was at Pauline's.

"'Madame has gone out,' said the footman; 'madame rides every morning, but madame will return at noon to breakfast. If madame's mother will be so kind as to wait for madame ——'

"That's how my daughter's servants are trained!

"I went into the small salon — I opened the window. I was so happy. I was going to see

Pauline come home on horseback. I had never seen her on horseback!

"At quarter to twelve a riding-habit turns the corner of the street. It was Pauline! Mounted on a horse that shone like silver in the sunlight and followed, as she was, by a tiger with such a distinguished air!

"She came near; she looked up, and, seeing me at the window, she cried out:

"'Oh! mamma! good-morning, mamma; how glad I am!'

"And remember, my dear friend, that I was bundled up like a scarecrow. I looked like an old witch.

"Oh! I tell you she has a heart, that child has, and not many in her position would recognize their mother out loud like that, in the street, before all the passers-by, and before such a distinguished looking little groom.

"She came in with her riding-skirt over her arm and her little man's hat. A love, she was, a perfect love!

"She threw herself into my arms.

"'Mamma! mamma! Well, is it all right for to-morrow?'

"I told her it was all right for to-day if she chose; and I told her Monsieur Cardinal's little scheme. I was a little uneasy. I said to myself:

"'That isn't going to be any fun for the little one, to leave her fine house and all her luxury, to bury herself in a hole with her father and mother.'

"But, no—not at all. She was enchanted, positively enchanted. To pass a week among the green fields would make her over, give her a good rest. She couldn't stand any more of the winter that had just passed. It wasn't always pleasant to be forced to amuse yourself all the time. It would be a pleasant change for her to come and be bored a little bit with us in the country. Then there was a lot of pretty little coaxing things, very prettily said, that reminded me of the Pauline of the old days.

"There was something else that tickled her to death—that was the disguise. To be dressed like a little bourgeoise!

"She didn't want to wait till the next day, but to go that very day, straight away, with me. She had a dinner-party that night that she hated to think of. This would help her out of it.

"Pauline sent for Hermance, her first lady's maid —she has two—and told her to pick out the simplest and quietest of all her dresses, and spread them all out on a couch in her dressing-room.

"We galloped through our lunch and then went up to see the dresses. None of them would do. Any one of them costumes would have drawn a crowd in Ribeaumont.

"Pauline ordered her landau and off we went to visit the dry goods shops and milliners.

"Pauline bought two or three dresses and as many hats. She thought it was splendid.

"'You'll see how pretty I'll be, mamma!'

She was struck of a heap at the low prices. She kept saying to the clerks:

"'You must be wrong; that ought to cost more than that.'

"I kept nudging her with my elbow; for it isn't worth while to say such things in shops.

"Our purchases all made, the carriage filled with packages, we were riding home, when Pauline cries out: 'And papa's present! What had I better give papa?'

"I had an inspiration. I says to her: 'Your sister gave your father a bust of Voltaire once, and he often says he'd like to have now a bust of another writer of that time. I don't remember the name. Ah! I have it. Jean-Jacques. Yes, but Jean-Jacques what? wait a minute. There's a street of the same name—the street where the post-office is—Jean-Jacques Rousseau, that's it.'

"We went along the boulevard to buy the bust and packed it away in the carriage with the thirty-nine franc dresses and the thirteen franc fifty hats.

"Then we went back, and while Hermance was packing a little trunk, Pauline dressed herself. She picked out a percale dress with little sweet peas and a straw hat with wild poppies. She was sweet enough to eat. We went down stairs and got into the landau, and we were just going to start, when Pauline strikes her forehead.

"'Oh! Mon Dieu, my dinner to-night! I forgot all about it, and the one to-morrow and the next day!'

"She sent the footman to call Hermance, and when Hermance came, she says to her:

"'You must write at once to the baron that I can't go to-night, that I am going to see mamma in the country. And write the same thing to Monsieur Georges for to-morrow and the same thing to the marquis for the next day.'

"'Very well, madame.'

"'Write a very nice note to Monsieur Georges. The two others you can write as you please, I don't care.'

"We started. I was a little staggered.

"'You tell your lady's maid to write to those gentlemen!' I says.

"'Oh! Hermance signs my name. They all believe I write the letters. Hermance writes better than I do; she's been governess in a great family; she never makes a mistake in spelling. But as for me! It's a little your fault, mamma. You were much more anxious to teach me dancing than spelling.

" ' Because I thought it was more useful and I was right. Would you be what you are if it hadn't been for the ballet? And see what spelling brings you to—to be your lady's maid !'

" Chattering thus on one thing and another, we reached Saint-Germain. There we shifted the trunk and Jean-Jacques Rousseau's bust into a hired cab. Half an hour more, and we were at Ribeaumont; Monsieur Cardinal opened his arms to his daughter, but he called her his niece, because our little maid was there.

" Such a dinner ! such an evening ! Family life ! My dream !

" After dinner, we rearranged the salon to hang Jean - Jacques Rousseau opposite Voltaire. And then I sat down to a game of bézique with Pauline, just a small game, at two sous the thousand. It made me ten years younger to play bézique with my child.

" Monsieur Cardinal watched us. He put his work out of his hands to do it. After dinner in the evening is the time when he writes the journal of his life.

"He carried his good humor so far as to say he'd like to play two or three games with Pauline himself.

"Sometimes he condescends to play with me, he knows it makes me so happy. And it's a great concession for him to play bézique, for there is one thing in the game that exasperates him, and that's the *four kings, eighty*. There was a time when he wouldn't try to get them; he'd throw the kings away for the pleasure of throwing them away so as not to have to count them. But lately he's found a way. Now he plays for the *four kings*, but he never says the words. He says: *four what's-his-names, eighty*. That straightens out everything.

" At ten o'clock I gave them some tea, and some little cakes that I make myself. Pauline thought they were delicious. Indeed, she said something very imprudent; she cried out:

"'Oh! mamma, how good these little cakes are! I shouldn't have any better supper than this at the Café Anglais.'

"'Hum! hum!' says I.

"As luck would have it, Monsieur Cardinal didn't hear, leastways he made believe he didn't.

"After we'd drank our tea I took my Pauline into her little chamber, with white curtains. I helped her undress with my own hands. I was in my element again.

"You see, my dear friend, I don't have the same ideas on the subject of virtue that make Monsieur Cardinal so great. If I hadn't devoted myself, as I have, to my husband's existence, I'd think myself mighty well fixed to be Pauline's lady's maid. The next night I put her to bed myself and tucked her in with my own hands. That amused her, and she says to me: 'That's like it was when I was a youngster, mamma, do you remember? I was still in the crowd at the Opéra, and you and sister and I used to come home together after the play and have a jolly supper on six sous' worth of chestnuts from the stall on Boulevard des Batignolles.'

"Alas! my dear friend, for that happy day there was to be no to-morrow. The catastrophe is approaching.

"But, to explain how the catastrophe happened I shall have to go into details.

"There are some cavalry regiments in garrison at Saint-Germain, a league from here. Sometimes it's dragoons and sometimes chasseurs—just now it's chasseurs.

"As the country is very pretty out our way, the officers often ride along the road that passes our house.

"That always stirs up Monsieur Cardinal a little, because the regular army isn't in his platform. He don't acknowledge but one kind of army—the nation in arms. In time of peace, no soldiers. Gendarmes and gamekeepers Monsieur Cardinal consents to, especially since he's been a landowner in the country, where a crowd of vagabonds. are always robbing your hen-roosts. But no regular soldiers, no praetorian guards!

"Those are the words Monsieur Cardinal uses, and I repeat them to you just as he says them.

"In war time, my word! then it's another matter. Everybody's a soldier. Everyone has his musket and cartridges in his house. Those who have a horse go on horseback, and those who haven't got any horses go on foot, but everybody goes. That makes an army, but an army that isn't an army. It's a torrent, it's an avalanche!

"That's Monsieur Cardinal's kind of an army! It would be invincible. This is all fixed in Monsieur Cardinal's papers; he often tells me: 'I may die, Madame Cardinal, and everything is fixed in my papers.'

"In a quarter of an hour every citizen should be ready for any kind of a war, foreign or civil.

"Monsieur Cardinal hasn't neglected the slightest detail; for instance, for the artillery he's invented a plough that can be made into a cannon in five minutes. While we're at peace, it's a plough; war breaks out, it's a cannon. The farm hand becomes an artilleryman; every Sunday he practises two hours with his plough-cannon. It's a wonder!

"They don't have a single new minister of war— and they change them every three months!—that Monsieur Cardinal don't write and describe his discovery. Never a reply does he get! That don't astonish Monsieur Cardinal. It's what he calls the force of inertia in the departments.

"Now I'll tell you why I spoke about the regiments at Saint-Germain.

"Day before yesterday, about ten o'clock in the morning, Monsieur Cardinal was reading the newspapers in his study. He subscribes to nine newspapers—it's his one extravagance—eight of his way of thinking and one no end clerical. The last is to feed his anger, as he says.

"Pauline had gone out to take a little walk on the road, in a white muslin dress with a red rose stuck in her hair, and an old five sous straw hat of Monsieur Cardinal's on her head. She was bewitching!

"Monsieur Cardinal tried to stop her as she passed his study. He suggested reading his lecture on Voltaire to her, for as soon as he gets hold of anyone —— But the prospect didn't tempt Pauline.

"'No,' says she, 'as long as I'm in the country, I must get all the good I can out of the country, don't you see. I'm going for a walk in the fields.'

"'But do you know who Voltaire was?'

"'Yes, papa, he was a little wrinkled old man, that they used to have a statue of in the vestibule of the Théâtre-Français. They've put him up in the green-room in a jardinière. A regular monkey's head, but he don't look like a fool. There, you see, I know who Voltaire is.'

"With that she went out to walk, and I to the kitchen-garden to pick some strawberries. A country life, you know, and family life!

"All of a sudden I heard horses trotting along the road.

"'Confound it!' says I to myself, 'there's more of those monkeys of chasseurs; they'll stir Monsieur Cardinal all up, and disturb him in his work.'

"But the first thing I knew I heard shouts and roars of laughter in our yard.

"I looked out; Pauline was coming home followed by two officers of chasseurs on horseback. She'd met them on the road, and they both knew her, worse luck! She tried to get away from them but they chased her into the very yard of our house. She had rushed up to the top of the steps, and from there she sung out to them, half-laughing, half-angry:

"'Let me alone. Go away, go away!'

"'Come and breakfast with us now at Pavillon Henri IV.'

"'I don't say I won't some other day, but I can't to-day. Go away, go away!'

"But they wouldn't go away, and while I was hurrying up as fast as I could from the far end of the kitchen-garden, one of the two gentlemen began to ride his horse up the steps.

"And then, all of a sudden, out comes Monsieur Cardinal! It was just what I was afraid of, and I stood there as if I was struck by lightning, with my basket of strawberries in my hand.

"'Back, messieurs, back! This is my house.'

"'Come, papa, don't be angry. I know these gentlemen.'

"'But I don't know them!' cried Monsieur Cardinal, 'and I don't want to know them! Begone, messieurs, begone! A free citizen's house is no longer at the mercy of an unbridled soldiery! This recalls the blackest days of our history. Once more, messieurs, begone!'

"As he spoke, Monsieur Cardinal had his right arm stretched out in front of him. He was admirable! Motionless as a statue, and in such a theatrical attitude! The two officers must have been *comme il faut* fellows, for they rode away without saying a word after bowing to us women.

"To be sure Pauline—she had stayed on the stoop—was making behind Monsieur Cardinal's back the little imploring gesture that means, in the pantomime at the Opéra: 'Go away! Please go away!'

"So they went away, but after they'd gone, a frightful scene began.

"Monsieur Cardinal was hard, too hard, on Pauline. Then she lost her head; she's quick, you know.

"She told her father that those officers were very nice gentlemen, that one of them even belonged to the Jockey Club. She told him he had behaved like a vulgar idiot—yes, she said things a daughter ought not to say to her father.

"Monsieur Cardinal listened to it all in a sort of crushed way.

" I tried to stop Pauline, but I couldn't—she was all wound up. She ended by telling us she'd had enough of family life, she wasn't afraid to walk a league and she'd go and breakfast with those gentlemen at Pavillon Henri IV. And off she goes like a madwoman with her five-sou straw hat on her head.

" Then Monsieur Cardinal says to me as cool as a cucumber:

" 'I tried to give you back your daughter, Madame Cardinal,' says he, 'but I didn't succeed. Only one thing is left for me: politics! Let's go in, Madame Cardinal, let's go in.'

" We went in.

" He sat down and went at his newspapers again. His hand shook a little, but still he read. He has such energy, such force of will——

" In about quarter of an hour he looks up, he was quite calm again, and he says:

" 'You didn't notice the gesture I made just now from the stoop, to drive away those praetorians?'

" 'Oh! yes, you were superb!'

" 'Well, that was one of Mirabeau's favorite gestures.'

"What a man he is! my dear friend, what a man he is! Always thinking about his business, devoted to his political ideas, even at such moments!

"Your friend,

"ZOÉ CARDINAL."

VII

VIRGINIE CARDINAL

VII

VIRGINIE CARDINAL

"RIBEAUMONT, June 3, 1878.

"Ah! my dear friend, how much truth there is
in the proverb that declares that there ain't any
roses without thorns, nor any pleasure without
pain!

153

VII

VIRGINIE CARDINAL

RICHMOND, June 3, 1853.

Ah! my dear friend, how much truth there is
in the proverb that declares that there are no
roses without thorns, nor any pleasure without
pain.

VII

VIRGINIE CARDINAL

"RIBEAUMONT, June 3, 1878.

"Ah! my dear friend, how much truth there is in the proverb that declares that there ain't any roses without thorns, nor any pleasure without pain!

"It seems as if there was a fatality about it, and all Monsieur Cardinal's political triumphs are bound to be poisoned by his daughters' reckless actions.

"Six weeks ago it was Pauline. This time it's Virginie—yes, my dear Virginie, so reserved and reasonable and prudent and distinguished—she's made a fool of herself, a big fool of herself!

"However, everything's fixed all right, thanks to me, her mother; but such days as the 30th and 31st of May!

"I'll begin with the 30th. It was the day of the famous centenary, the day of the great lecture. It might have been about half-past seven or quarter to eight in the morning. I was just going over Monsieur Cardinal's manuscript, because I've learned the lecture by heart, too. I was to be seated, in the evening, right behind Monsieur Cardinal in the middle of the platform, and if he happened to get mixed up, why zip! I'd have been there to prompt him.

"I had just got to a passage against the priests, where he gives them a good dressing — although it don't suit my ideas. — You know I'm a little behindhand. I'd belong to the church if I wasn't afraid of vexing Monsieur Cardinal.

" Well, all of a sudden, just as I was in the midst of that fine nigging of the priests, there was a ring at the street door. I looked out—it was the telegraph boy. A despatch! Whenever a despatch comes, I think first of all of my two chicks.

" I wasn't mistaken — it was a despatch from Florence, from my son-in-law, the marquis.

" In my maternal uneasiness I began to read it aloud, without paying any attention to Monsieur Cardinal, who was right there :

" ' *Virginie gone. Not alone. Took express, arrive Paris May 30, one o'clock afternoon. I follow, next express. Arrive 31, same hour. Prevent Virginie going farther.*'

" ' I don't understand!' says Monsieur Cardinal.

" And I must go and sing out like the old fool I am :

" ' Ah ! I understand only too well. Not alone ! Not alone !—A mother's heart is never mistaken. Virginie has run away with a lover !'

"That slipped out of my mouth. I didn't think of Monsieur Cardinal, how delicate and squeamish he is about his honor. He turned white as a sheet.

"'I had two daughters,' says he, 'one that turned out well and another that turned out ill, and now the one that turned out well is beginning to turn out ill too.'

"That sentence, written down, don't seem to mean much, my dear friend, but when Monsieur Cardinal said it, if you knew how impressive and dramatic it was!

"Just then, by good luck, I had an inspiration. I took up the despatch again and pretended to read it over carefully, and then I said:

"'I'm crazy. It ain't that at all. It ain't anything of any consequence. See here, Monsieur Cardinal, just listen a minute. This is what happened at Florence. There's been some family quarrel between Virginie and the marquis. At that she starts off—without so much as a by your leave—a hot-headed performance! The marquis rushes off after her by the next train, to catch her and beg her

pardon,—and he must be in the wrong, must the
marquis, for he's a dignified man, and he wouldn't
run after our girl if she'd run off with a lover, you
know.'

"But Monsieur Cardinal wasn't convinced. He
was turning that despatch inside out, and he says
to me :

"'"Not alone? not alone?" How do you explain
those words, Madame Cardinal ?'

"Then I had another inspiration.

"'Not alone—why that means that Virginie has
her maid with her. The marquis put those words
in, so that we shouldn't worry. And then, look
here, Monsieur Cardinal, this makes it absolutely
certain. Not alone—*Pas seule*,—look, is in the femi-
nine, because of the *e* at the end. Well, if Virginie
had gone with a lover it would be in the masculine.
It would be *Pas seul.*'

"This last argument made Monsieur Cardinal
quite easy in his mind.

"I told him not to worry, to stay quietly at
home, digging away at his speech, and I went off to
Paris.

" I went to the station of the Lyon railway and asked which way passengers from Florence would come in, and they told me. Then I planted myself right there in front of the gate and waited anxiously.

" I didn't have long to wait. I saw my Virginie in the crowd, pale and trembling, with a veil over her face, hanging on the arm of a tall fellow, a regular lady-killer with great black moustaches and curly hair.

" She saw me, dropped the tall fellow's arm and rushed up to me, shrieking :

" ' O mamma ! mamma !'

" My fingers fairly itched. I was getting ready to give her a couple of cuffs—that was my system long ago at the Opéra—when lo and behold my Virginie throws herself into my arms, bursts out sobbing, and says :

" ' If you only knew, mamma; I've had enough of it already !'

" Meantime the lady-killer came up, and he says in a sort of Italian gibberish :

" ' Coma, Virginie ——'

"'Excuse me, monsieur,' says I, looking him right in the whites of his eyes, 'excuse me, I'm her mother.'

"'Yes,' says Virginie, 'this is mamma. Will you allow me to speak to her?'

"'Vera well. I go to look after ze baggazhe.'

"And he went, and well for him he did, for if he hadn't he'd have got the two cuffs.

"I took Virginie off one side to a bench, and I said to her :

"'Come, who's this clown?'

"Then I learned the truth, and horrible it was, my dear friend.

"An Italian tenor! he was an Italian tenor!

"To be a marchioness, to take up with a lover, and not to take him out of her own set! It was too much to believe, but it was a fact!

"While the fellow was off looking after his luggage, the poor little kitten told me the whole story: how bored she was at Florence; that her great amusement was the theatre, and last winter there was a tenor with a beautiful voice and fascinating in love songs.

"She met this tenor several times at parties in the best society. The last time, at one of her friends', a princess's, she was alone with him for five minutes in a window recess. And there my gentleman had the impudence to make a declaration of love, saying that it was all right for him to talk to her that way, as he had no hope, as he was going to London the next day for the season, and should never see her again. At that she was so upset that she fainted away right before all the first Italian society !

"You can imagine the scandal.

"The marquis took her away and made an outrageous scene when they got back to the palace, carrying his cruelty so far that he did not stop short of accusing her of being the tenor's mistress; she cried out:

"'It ain't true! that ain't true!'

"And then he flies into a devil of a rage and begins to beat her, as if she was so much plaster. Slaps and thwacks, if you please, with his open hand, my word!—He left her in a dead faint on a couch and went out, saying:

Chapter Seven

VIRGINIE CARDINAL

"After the lecture Monsieur Cardinal was escorted home in triumph with torches ; the band marched ahead and played patriotic tunes."

"'Understand, madame, I don't propose to be the laughing-stock of Florence!'

"She was left alone. She had a fit of rage too.

"'Ah! you don't want to be the laughing-stock of Florence, don't you? Well, you wait! just wait a bit!'

"And she ran away, in her ball dress, after she'd taken pains to take off all her diamonds and jewelry, everything that was worth anything. She went off without a sou or a jewel or anything.

"She went to the tenor's room. She said to him:

"'Here I am,—you love me, I love you—let us go!'

"So they started. But they were hardly in the cars before Virginie felt that she was in a fair way to make a fool of herself. Ah! it don't take an intelligent woman long to go all round a tenor!

"At last the tenor appeared again. He had had his baggage loaded on a little omnibus, and came to get Virginie.

"He was going to take the express for Boulogne. He was only going to cross Paris. But I had my child and I didn't let her go. I was like a lioness defending her young ones, and when he had the cheek to say to Virginie:

"'Coma, I haf ze leetle omnibousse.'

"I answered him:

"'You can just get into your little *omnibousse* all by your little self, and pretty quick, too, my boy. I'll give you marchionesses to amuse you during your London season! Come, off you go for the Gare du Nord, and quicker than that!'

"He tried to kick, but I went on:

"'No nonsense, or I'll make a fuss. You haven't got any claim on her and I have, you know. All the mothers 'll be on my side, and all the police-men!'

"A crowd was beginning to collect. Virginie was trembling like a leaf She begged him to go and at last he got into his little omnibus all alone. He went off to take his train to London. I got into a cab with Virginie and we started for the Saint-Lazare station.

"As soon as we were in the cab, I says to Virginie:

"'The first thing we've got to think about is not the marquis, but your father. We mustn't let anything disturb Monsieur Cardinal—to-day of all days. To-night's his lecture on Voltaire. It happens bad, you see; you've taken a bad time to get into such a mess. Any other day it wouldn't have made so much matter. But we'll try to get out of it all the same. Your father mustn't suspect your virtue. That's the main point. We must pile everything on to the marquis.'

"'But that will be lying, mamma.'

"'Oh! there you are with your delicate feelings. Yes, it will be lying, but anything's allowable when Monsieur Cardinal's peace of mind and honor are at stake.'

"We got home at last. I rushed into Monsieur Cardinal's study.

"'She's here,' I said, 'she's an angel—and he, the man's a monster. He beat her—beat her till the blood came!'

"'Nothing surprises me that a clerical can do.— Come, my Virginie, come, poor martyr!'

"He held out his arms to her.

" She hesitated about jumping into them.

" ' You're too good, papa, I did wrong —— '

" Mere delicacy, you know, absurd delicacy! I cut her short. I pushed her into Monsieur Cardinal's arms, and then I put a stop to the touching scene.

" Monsieur Cardinal didn't have any time to waste on emotion on such a day. He needed all his strength for the evening.

" So I says to Virginie :

" ' Come. Let's leave your father—don't excite him. The marquis will be in Paris to-morrow, and he'll come and beg you from your parents on both knees.'

" Such a day, my dear! I kept running from Monsieur Cardinal to Virginie and from Virginie to Monsieur Cardinal. She made me uneasy, did Virginie. She had the ideas of a different class. She made too much of what she'd done, she thought the marquis wouldn't forgive her, she wanted to go to London and join the other.

" ' There's a *corps de ballet* at Covent Garden,' she said, ' and I'll join it. I'll go back to dancing.'

"'A marchioness on the boards!'

"'Oh! no, mamma, I'll take my maiden name again.'

"'Your father's name! You think of dragging Monsieur Cardinal's name back on the boards! Ah! never, not much! If you go to making a fool of yourself, you'll do it in the marquis's name and not in your father's!'

"As she kept bothering me with that sort of nonsense, that night when it came time to go to the lecture with Monsieur Cardinal, I just turned the key on her in case she should take a fancy to try some new freak.

"Well, I got to the lecture room, and it was very fine, my dear friend, very fine! All Ribeaumont was there. But alas! there was nothing but Ribeaumont. And yet Monsieur Cardinal had sent tickets to all the Paris papers. Not one came. There's your Parisians and their contempt for the provinces!

"Monsieur Cardinal had had the two busts of Voltaire and Jean-Jacques Rousseau put on the platform, Pauline's and Virginie's presents. They

were on two imitation marble columns. Monsieur
Cardinal sat in the middle; he had a very fine
passage on that: that he was the bond of union
between those two great men and was going to
bring them together. It seems that, when they
were alive, they couldn't bear each other and passed
their time saying hard things about each other.
It's only since they've been dead that they've been
going along together and the two have made a
pair.

"I don't know whether Monsieur Cardinal's lecture had much effect. It wasn't effect exactly, but
something better: astonishment, stupefaction. Monsieur Cardinal expected that.

" The night before, when he was reading over his
lecture, he says to me:

"'It's too much for them. They won't understand it, but this time I'm speaking to a larger
audience, to France, to Europe. This is something
I shall have printed.'

" To have something printed, to see his name on
the cover of a book—that's another of Monsieur
Cardinal's ambitions!

"Well, he was right, Monsieur Cardinal was right, as he always is. I don't think they understood much of his lecture, but they applauded, and the less they understood the more they applauded. They were glad to hear things out of their range, above their heads; it flattered them to tell themselves that he'd made that for them; they didn't understand, but it made them all the prouder to think he'd thought they would be capable of understanding things so much above them.

"By the way, the same thing that happened to them happened to me one night at the Théâtre-Français on Rue de Richelieu. Monsieur Cardinal wanted me to see a tragedy.

"He'd been saying to me for a long time:

"'Madame Cardinal, you really must hear a tragedy at the Théâtre-Français.'

"So one night we went together. It didn't amuse me much, I must confess; but there were some long speeches that the actors spouted without taking breath—you felt that they said it well, you felt that there were fine thoughts underneath it. I was bored, oh! yes, I was, my word! But I pretended to admire it all the same, with the best of them.

"After the lecture Monsieur Cardinal was escorted home in triumph with torches; the band marched ahead and played patriotic tunes.

"There wouldn't have been a happier evening in my whole life if I hadn't been thinking all the time of my little chick that I'd left under lock and key at home.

"I had the satisfaction to find her well calmed down and quieted; her natural dignity was on top again. She saw that there was nothing for her to do but return and take her place in Florence, that she had no right to compromise her father's name in love affairs. She had made up her mind to become a good, faithful wife once more, so far as it was possible.

"The next day we both went to Paris.

"My first idea was to make the marquis come and ask Monsieur Cardinal for Virginie again; but, on thinking it over, that plan seemed to have more against it than for it; they couldn't have helped having an explanation, and that would give a shock to Monsieur Cardinal, who knew nothing about Virginie's prank with that mountebank of a tenor.

"So I arranged something else that was much better and succeeded splendidly. Ah! such critical times as that give a mother ingenuity and cunning, I don't care what she is. Virginie and I had our breakfast at a restaurant near the Lyon station. At quarter to one I says to Virginie:

"'You wait right here; I'll go alone and meet the marquis. You mustn't let it seem as if you wanted to jump down his throat. We must never admit that we're in the wrong—especially when we are.'

"At one o'clock I was in the station waiting for the husband on the same spot where I had waited for—the other one, the day before!

"Ah! I saw at once that we could do whatever we wanted to with the marquis, that he wouldn't weigh an ounce. He turned pale when he saw me alone, and cried out:

"'Virginie! Virginie!'

."He called her by her pet name still! We were safe! He was still in love!

"I'm nothing but a big fool, I know — I don't make any mistake about that; but I've always had one gift—it was my specialty at the Opéra.   I can tell instantly whether a man's in love or not—so much so that other mothers often asked my advice about their daughters.

"'Madame Cardinal,' they'd say, 'you've got such a sharp eye, just come and look—we want to know what you think about it.'

"So then I'd go and look and I'd tell them: 'That man is stuck!' or else the other way: 'No, that isn't real love, it's only fancy.'

"In short, I had a keen scent for such things. I know that that sort of thing wouldn't happen at the Opéra to-day, it would happen in society.   But love is the same thing, always and everywhere. Whether it's for a ballet-girl or a marchioness love always makes a man the same big idiot, and that's a fact.

"I had the marquis: his first look was for Virginie, I had him in my grip.   If Virginie had been there everything could have been fixed up in a second, without a word; she'd only have had to show herself to get back all her power. But I didn't dare risk it.

"I was afraid of a scene before a lot of people. You see I'd caused a little excitement in the station with the tenor the day before, and if I'd raised another row the next day they'd have said

"'Well, well! who's this fat old woman that comes here every morning making a rumpus with passengers by the Florence express?'

"I set the marquis's mind at rest and told him Virginie was safe under my wing. I made him sit down on the same bench where I'd confessed Virginie the day before, and we had an explanation. It was a hot one, I tell you! As soon as he knew Virginie was all right he undertook to be high and mighty with me. He set out to tell me that he'd never see Virginie again, that he came to Paris just to arrange things decently, that he was ready to make her a handsome allowance —and he repeated his famous remark about not wanting to be the laughing-stock of Florence. Then I let out at him. I had reason enough, my dear friend.

"'The laughing-stock of Florence, indeed! My word! when your first wife was alive, that was when you were the laughing-stock of Florence! And you came to Paris to look for consolation in the corps de ballet. She was bored to death, was your first wife, bored to death! But she was a society woman and it's a merit in them to have lovers. In our girls, it's a crime! There's your society! Ah! Monsieur Cardinal was right in wanting to make it over from top to bottom. If you'd taken Virginie out of a convent, it would have been all right for her to deceive you, to have lovers by the handful; it wouldn't surprise anybody, it would be in the order of things and you'd invite her lovers to dinner! And they'd be your intimate friends! But just because you've taken a poor girl from the Opéra, from the ballet, she isn't allowed to do anything—and because she happened to come from Florence by the same train with a beast of a tenor, you bellow as if you were being skinned. What do you suppose happened on an express train that goes twenty leagues an hour and paltry stops of ten minutes now and then? I tell you,—

I, her mother, — that nothing happened at all!
What's the first thing to be done? To avoid scandal.
That's why you're going to take Virginie back,
and right away too. I don't want scandal any
more than you do, because it would come back on
Monsieur Cardinal, and it mustn't come back on
Monsieur Cardinal. So if you don't take Virginie
back there'll be a row. Do you know what she'll
do? She'll go back to the ballet, she'll go on
the stage again, she'll make a fool of herself, and
not under the respected name of Monsieur Cardinal.
Oh! no! never fear—but under your name, yours.
When a young girl is married, her freaks don't
concern her family, but her husband. And that's
when you'll be the laughing-stock of Florence!'

"As I saw that this last argument touched him,
I tried a little sentiment on him.

"'Virginie is within two steps,' I says. 'Come.
You must open your arms to each other. She's
been to blame, perhaps, but so have you. It was
the first time she'd ever been struck by anybody
but her mother. That upset the poor child. Say,
if it embarrasses you to go back to Florence alone

with her, how would you like to have me go along with you? It would be hard for me to leave Monsieur Cardinal, but I'll do it all the same. And when the first Italian society sees Virginie come back on her mother's arm, I'd like to know who'll dare to kick! Your minxes in Florence would find they had somebody to reckon with!'

"He was more and more shaken. He told me that if he went back with Virginie, he preferred to go alone with her, that he didn't need me—in short, quarter of an hour afterward they were in each other's arms. After that they took rooms at the Grand Hotel for a month. That was my idea, too. They had a suite on the first floor facing the boulevard. They showed themselves together everywhere, at the Bois and the theatres. They gave great dinner parties. Their presence in Paris was noticed by the newspapers in the *Echoes of Society* columns. The notices were copied into the Italian papers, and Florence thought it was only a fit of temper.

"That night I returned to Ribeaumont, and that terrible day came to an end in the tranquillity of the domestic fireside, beside Monsieur Cardinal, who was correcting the proofs of his lecture. But I don't care, it was too much for a wife and a mother to have to endure at one time.

" Yours, with all my heart,

" ZOÉ CARDINAL."

VIII

THE FIREWORKS

VIII

THE FIREWORKS

" RIBEAUMONT, May 5, 1880.

" More excitement, my dear friend; Monsieur Cardinal's life is a real drama.   These last two years,
since his famous lecture on the centenary of Voltaire,
he's been pining away, devouring himself, consuming

179

Ch. Léandre inv   L. Müller sc.

VIII

THE FIREWORKS

"RIBEAUMONT, May 5, 1880.

"More excitement, my dear friend; Monsieur Cardinal's life is a real drama. These last two years, since his famous lecture on the centenary of Voltaire, he's been pining away, devouring himself, consuming

179

himself. He has sent in fifty petitions for office. He has written more than ten times to the deputy of our district. Never an answer! In his last letter to the deputy, he suggested the creation of a new office that would suit him well: *Inspector-General of the Minds of the Rural Population.* The duties would consist in arousing the country districts from their apathy. Nothing, not even a word to say it was received!

" At last Monsieur Cardinal lost his temper.

" He took his pen and wrote the deputy one of the stinging letters that nobody else can write like him: that it had ceased to be a joke; that a man chosen to office under universal suffrage couldn't have anything to do with such an indifferent creature; and that it was hardly worth while to waste one's strength helping elect a deputy, if that deputy wouldn't pay the least attention to the affairs of his electors.

" That time Monsieur Cardinal got an answer, but such an answer! Here it is, word for word

" ' Monsieur: I advise you to dispense with writing to me so often. If you want to know why I don't reply, go to the office of the prefecture and try to put an end to reports that are not favorable to you.'

"Reports not favorable to Monsieur Cardinal! You can imagine that he flared up at that.

"'I know where this comes from,' he cried; 'the Jesuits! I recognize the hand of the Jesuits! They are intriguing against me, but I'll foil them!'

"He insisted on going to the prefecture that very day, and wanted me to go with him. He proposed to put his slanderers to shame before me. We had our pony harnessed into our little basket wagon — Virginie's last birthday present to Monsieur Cardinal — and started for Versailles together.

"We arrived and got hold of an usher impudence itself.

"'Monsieur le Préfet,' said Monsieur Cardinal.

"'Monsieur le Préfet don't receive,' replied the usher, without raising his eyes, and kept on reading his paper, a reactionary paper.

"'He'll receive me!'

"'No more than anybody else.'

"'I beg you to be more courteous. You don't know who I am.'

"'Who are you?'

"'Monsieur Cardinal, Municipal Councillor of Ribeaumont. A Republican prefect should always be at the service of the representatives of the people chosen by universal suffrage.'

"My word! the usher, without even answering, coolly began to turn his paper. No one has any idea of the impudence of those fellows as soon as they get a place.

"At that Monsieur Cardinal broke out. He told the usher that he'd have him kicked out, that he would see the prefect.

"I tried to calm him. No use. He shrieked and stormed.

"A door opened. A little light-haired young man came out.

"'What's the matter? What's all this row about?'

"'I'm a Municipal Councillor,' says Monsieur Cardinal. 'Here's what the deputy of my arrondissement writes me. I come here to grind the slanders into dust.'

"He was very soft and polite, was the little light-haired fellow.

"He shows us into his office, and he says to
Monsieur Cardinal:

"'I'll look at the files in your case.'

"They brought him Monsieur Cardinal's file in a
blue cover. It was a huge thing. It contained
all his petitions for places. Monsieur Cardinal
recognized them at a distance, and I saw,—from a
distance, too—a thick letter written on paper with
Prefecture de Police printed on it.

"The young fellow began to read that letter and
Monsieur Cardinal and I both saw as plainly as
could be that he was trying not to laugh.

"'What is it?' Monsieur Cardinal asked him.

"'Nothing, nothing, it's nothing.'

"'You laughed internally, monsieur. I am entitled to know why you laughed internally. I am
entitled to know what there is in my file.'

"'It's a confidential letter.'

"'There can't be any confidential letters so far
as I'm concerned. I have lived in broad daylight,
under the eyes of my fellow-citizens. I have fought
and suffered for my country. I won't go away from
here till I've read that letter. Give it to me!'

"'Ah! you tire me out at last!' cried the little fellow. 'Here—read it—if you insist upon knowing. That's why your petitions haven't been answered.'

" He handed the letter to Monsieur Cardinal, who said to me:

"'I need my glasses. Read it, Madame Cardinal.'

"'No,' said the little clerk, very hastily, 'there's no need to make madame read it.'

" At that Monsieur Cardinal said one of the things that pay a poor creature like me for all her sacrifice, all her devotion, all her abnegation.

"'Madame Cardinal has been the faithful and brave companion of my whole life. I never have had and never will have any secrets from her. Read, Madame Cardinal, read.'

" The little fellow made a gesture, as much as to say: 'Oh! well, let them fix it to suit themselves,'— and I began.

" Here are the horrible things I read, my dear friend, here they are:

"'*Sieur Cardinal is a person of doubtful moral character* ——'

" Indignation choked me, strangled me. I wanted
to stop.

" Monsieur Cardinal, very calm and dignified,
said : 'Go on—go on,'—with the air of authority
that belongs to him alone. I went on :

" ' *And his means of support seem to be derived
?from an impure source.*'

" I wanted to stop again, but I felt my arm
gripped as if it was in a vise. It was Monsieur
Cardinal's hand—and he says to me in a firm voice :

" ' Madame Cardinal, I order you to go on to
the end, without pausing.'

" Ah! my dear friend, when you haven't seen
Monsieur Cardinal at such moments you haven't
seen anything, you don't know what coolness
means, and self-control.

" I went on :

" ' *He has two daughters who have danced at
the Opéra. The older lives abroad in concubinage
with an Italian marquis. The younger, under the
name of Pauline de Giraldas, lives a life of ;pleasure
on a grand scale.*'

" Yes, my dear, I had the strength to read those things aloud before Monsieur Cardinal. Virginie in concubinage!—when she's a marchioness as regular as any noodle in Faubourg Saint-Germain.—And Pauline living a life of pleasure on a grand scale! It would be mighty convenient for her to be on a long ladder, for ——

" Monsieur Cardinal got up out of his chair right after that foolish thing about the ladder, and said to the little fellow, with wonderful calmness :

" 'I won't stoop, monsieur, to discuss such slanders. Where does this information come from? From the police—that is to say, from a commissioner of police appointed under the empire. That deprives the document of all value. I withdraw, but you shall hear from me, you and your government! Come, Madame Cardinal, come!'

" We went out, and on the stairs I said to him :

" 'Why didn't you answer for Virginie? You could answer for Virginie.'

" 'Yes, Madame Cardinal, I could answer for Virginie, but I couldn't for Pauline. In that case it was better to make a simple, plain denial of the whole thing. It's more dignified—it has more effect!'

"Would you believe it: when we got home, Monsieur Cardinal weakened, gave up for the first time in his life.

" He dropped into a chair, saying :

"'It's all over, I give up! What's the use of sacrificing one's self for one's country, scattering one's affections to the winds, and acting the true Brutus toward one's children? This is my reward!'

"I was going to take the ball on the bound and propose to him to come and have a nice little dinner at Pauline's. But he had already recovered all his energy and was stalking up and down the room.

"'No, I never will give up, never! Universal suffrage is at hand to avenge me. There's an election to the General Council in three months. I hesitated to come forward on account of the expense. I was going to give way to the mayor, that Orléanist in disguise. I'll make a fight for it and take it from him. I'll resort to any means. I'll be elected. I'll think it all out to-night, and to-morrow I'll have my plan all made.'

" Neither Monsieur Cardinal nor I slept that night.

" He was thinking up his plan and I was tormented and uneasy in my mind. I questioned myself, I went over my whole past life, and I said to myself:

" ' Madame Cardinal, have you done your duty? Can it be true? hasn't Monsieur Cardinal's life been honorable? If it hasn't, you, his wife, are to blame. You ought to have prevented him from living that way, if it wasn't proper.' But the farther down I went into my conscience, the calmer I found it.

" They say there's only one rule of morals — that's nonsense invented by folks with a hundred thousand francs a year. There's as many ways of being moral as there are people. Ah! if Monsieur Cardinal had been an ordinary man, I should have been wrong; but as long as Monsieur Cardinal was what he was, who would have the face to blame me for doing what I done? The first thing to do was to make sure of Monsieur Cardinal's peace. His character and his ideas were too lofty to stoop to the work of a petty clerk. He was too proud to resign himself to earn his living miserably in inferior places. He was only fitted for great places where there'd be something to manage, some one to order round. So it was his wife's and his children's duty to stir about and make him independent, so that he could use his great talents, and that's what we did!

" The next morning, Monsieur Cardinal's plan was all ready.

" The mayor was making a worse use than ever of his money. The past week he had married off one of his daughters, and the next Sunday he gave a great party in his park. Fireworks in the evening, and during the day the greased pole, sack races, pig races, candy passed round and handfuls of sous tossed to the youngsters of the Commune— the whole thing sickened Monsieur Cardinal! He said they were infamous customs borrowed from a shameful period in our history, called feudality.

" Monsieur Cardinal's plan was to give a great dinner to all the members of the Municipal Council except the mayor, the next Sunday, and to have some fine fireworks, but not just for the children, for the men too: fireworks that would have a philosophical and political meaning: fireworks that would be an entertainment and a demonstration at the same time.

"Friday morning I started for Paris, I had a heap of things to buy for the dinner two days later, and the fireworks to order.

"Monsieur Cardinal had written everything down in a note I was to give to Monsieur Ruggieri, marked:

"'*Memorandum for anticlerical fireworks.*'

"'The bouquet at the close to be replaced by a set piece, a structure representing a primary school, and on top of the structure, in great letters of fire this inscription:

"'DOWN WITH THE JESUITS!'

"I reached Paris. I went to Rue Montorgueil to order my fish and chickens, and then I went to Pauline's. I found her all alone.

"'I don't disturb you?'

"'You, mamma? never. I'm expecting the prince, but that don't make any difference; I'll introduce you to him.   He'll be delighted to make your acquaintance.'

"'A prince!'

"'Yes, and a real one; not a prince to laugh at, no, a prince of one of the oldest courts in Europe, and very close to the throne.   He said to me yester-day: "There are only two persons between me and the throne."   He'll be here in a minute.   You'll see what a nice little fellow he is.   Let's play bézique while we're waiting.'

"We were in the middle of our fourth game of bézique when all of a sudden the door opened.   A tall footman in knee-breeches and silk stockings announced: 'His Highness.'

"Yes, my dear friend, he's that intimate with Pauline!   And, no matter what you say, it makes a mother's heart beat!

"Well, in comes His Highness.

"A real *gamin*.   Not twenty years old, light hair and fresh cheeks.

"'Monseigneur, this is mamma!' says Pauline.

"Ah! I tell you the little fellow's mighty well-bred —for it wasn't the first time one of my daughters had introduced me to a prince—that happened several times at supper-parties in the old Opéra days, for I never used to leave my children except at the last extremity—but I never flattered myself, and I always noticed that the princes would have been just as well pleased if I hadn't been there. They'd make a little face I understood very well, as much as to say: 'Bah! the mother, we've got to swallow the mother!'

"Well, this youngster didn't make up any face. He was delightful. He bowed as a man should to a lady, whoever she is, and said with the funniest little accent you ever heard:

"'Dear Madame Cardinal!'

"And I thought to myself that he must be mad with love for Pauline to be as polite as that to me—because there's another thing I've noticed, in my career as a mother, and that is that I could always reckon a man's love for my daughters by the amount of respect he had for their mother. I've often said to Virginie:

"'Take care, my child, look out, that man don't love you sincerely. He isn't polite enough to your mother.'

" But the prince was.

" ' Pray, don't let me disturb you,' he says; 'go on with your bézique!'

" We kept on playing.   He stood behind Pauline and she consulted him: *'Would you throw that away, monseigneur?'* And from time to time she'd let slip some little familiarity, like: *'How stupid you are!'* or *'You don't know anything about the game!'* And every time she had four kings, she announced: *Four papas, eighty*—giving him a sly look—a delicate allusion to her condition.

" And they were both so happy, they laughed so happily when the *Four papas, eighty* came around again!   Ah! youth is beautiful! and love is beautiful!

" For my part, I was in my element.   I let the time go by.   I forgot what time it was,—so that all of a sudden I raised my head and looked at the clock—Four o'clock.

" I had told Monsieur Cardinal I'd take the train at half-past four.   He was going to meet me at the station at Saint-Germain with our little pony-cart. Make Monsieur Cardinal wait—never on my life!

Not even to stay with a prince, because, after all, a prince is only a prince, a man who owes everything to his birth, while Monsieur Cardinal's a man who owes nothing to anybody but himself.

"I had forgot all about the fireworks and I didn't have time to go to Monsieur Ruggieri's.

"I told Pauline about it. That was where the prince showed what a charming man he was. He undertook to do it for me. But I had to tell him, and him the heir of a royal family, that our fireworks was to have a slap at the Jesuits, and I gave him Monsieur Cardinal's note. He read it and thought it was very original, very original.

"There was another thing that embarrassed me; that was about the price.

"It made me a little sheepish to let that young fellow pay for fireworks that could hardly suit his ideas. But as soon as I started to open my mouth on the subject, Pauline says:

"'You're a great stupid, mamma; let the prince do it. It's nothing of any consequence, that silly thing.'

"I didn't insist, in the first place because I've always thought it was absurd to pay yourself for things somebody else was willing to pay for. That's one of the principles I taught my little girls.

"I went back to Ribeaumont. I found Monsieur Cardinal at the station. I told him I had ordered everything, chickens, fish, cakes, fireworks, and that it would all arrive Sunday morning. And arrive it did.

"Two of Monsieur Ruggieri's men brought down the fireworks—splendid fireworks that filled a whole wagon and must have cost at least a thousand francs.

"Monsieur Cardinal came down to the garden a minute to show the place where the fireworks was to be set up; but he was very busy, was Monsieur Cardinal, and he went right back to his study, because he'd had another idea in the night.

"His idea was to give a toast in the English fashion at the dinner—to make a *spitche*—that's the word they use over there. Monsieur Cardinal knows a heap of words in all languages now. This *spitche*, which he was going to deliver off-hand in the evening, Monsieur Cardinal was writing out, and then he'd got to learn it by heart. It seems

that they have a way of talking over in England
that isn't like ours.   It isn't eloquence, it's conversation, *humourre*, another word Monsieur Cardinal used, for he'd like to introduce that kind of
political talks in France.

"At half-past six they sat down to dinner.   Everything went off splendidly.

"The dinner was fine: fish, chickens, everything
was all right.

"Monsieur Cardinal's *spitche* made a tremendous
hit, and at half-past nine they went down into the
garden for the fireworks.   They began to go off in
great shape.   Pin-wheels, Bengal fire, rockets, gush-
ing fountains, nothing missed fire; and you know,
there's generally a lot of things that do miss in a
fireworks' show.   The weather was all anyone could
ask: no moon and no wind.   All of a sudden a
building of fire appeared among the trees.   It was
the set piece.   You could see the pillars and a
door.

"Everybody exclaimed:

"'Oh! how lovely it is!   How much better than
the mayor's!'

"'Wait!' cried Monsieur Cardinal, 'wait, this is nothing! Wait till you see the pediment! wait for the inscription!'

"The pediment appeared; the inscription lighted up, but what a frightful thing!

"What do you suppose was written in letters of fire on top of the building? Instead of: '*Down with the Jesuits!*' it was

"Vive l'Empereur!

"How did it happen? I don't know yet. Was it a joke of the little prince's, did he think it would be fun to send us some Bonapartist fireworks, instead of anticlerical? I can't believe that of such a distinguished young man who's so fond of Pauline. Was it a mistake of Monsieur Ruggieri's? It's a great big establishment where they must have fireworks to suit all sorts of opinions. They might have made a slight mistake. Or it may be, they wanted to work off some old thing they had in stock. They must have had lots of fireworks on hand at the fall of the Empire. That wouldn't be very nice of them, and come to think of it, it can't be so, for they must have thought we'd notice it.

"However, when they saw those words blazing out:

VIVE L'EMPEREUR!

the crowd began to yell and hiss. They ain't Bonapartists in that region.

"Monsieur Cardinal threw himself into the middle of the fire like a lion.

"The workmen yelled to him :

"'Don't go near it! Don't go near it! You're not used to it, you'll get hurt!'

"But he didn't hear anything. He was crazy with rage. He tried to upset the whole concern. I rushed into the flames after him. I pulled him out. The ends of my false hair, my curls and the bows of my cap were all singed.

"All the guests went away in a rage. Monsieur Cardinal ran after them.

"'Come back! come back!' he shouted. 'Let me explain. It ought to have been : "*Down with the Jesuits!*"'

"But nobody would listen.

"So Monsieur Cardinal and I went back alone. He fell in a heap on a bench. Then, when I saw him in that state of collapse, I mustered up some courage for once in my life, and I gave Monsieur Cardinal a little talking to.

"'Listen to me,' says I, 'if this is the end of your political ambition, perhaps this mistake about the fireworks is a blessing from Heaven. Perhaps it's written on high that you weren't cut out for politics. Oh! I know you don't believe in things being written on high, but I do, myself, I'm just weak enough. I tell you, Monsieur Cardinal, you're too stiff-backed in your principles. Politics is made for clowns, for merry-Andrews, for men who change their opinions every week. It isn't made for you, because you never change yours.

"'Who's the man that ought to have got everything? You! And who's the man that's got nothing? You! Under the Empire you used to say:

"'"After the Empire, I shall get there!"

"'The Empire fell, and you didn't get anywhere.

"'Then you said:

"'" After MacMahon it will be my turn."

"'And what did they give you after MacMahon?
Nothing at all.   You consoled yourself by saying:

"'" I can't expect anything from those fellows of
the Left Centre.   But when Gambetta's at the head
of affairs I shall have all I want!"

"'Well, Gambetta's there, and what comes to
your pocket? Insults from his office-holders! All
these people are the same, you see, whether their
name's Napoléon or MacMahon or Gambetta. They
all have the same routine and the same prejudices.
They'll never understand the greatness of your
character. They'll always be throwing your daughters at your head. Your daughters! your daughters! Well, perhaps they're right after all. Come,
Monsieur Cardinal, let me tell you what I think
once for all. I have common feelings, to be sure,
bourgeois ideas, but this is what I think: that your
true career isn't politics; your true career's your
daughters!'

"There I stopped, frightened at what I'd said.
But Monsieur Cardinal had become quiet, almost
smiling, and he said, good-naturedly:

"'I don't blame you. Madame Cardinal, you can't understand all your words mean—but nothing shall get the better of my energy. Everything turns against me, even my fireworks. Monsieur Gambetta's government has no use for me? Very good—I'll be patient. I'll wait. Universal suffrage is a fact. My turn will come.'

"Just as Monsieur Cardinal finished speaking, I saw the sergeant of the gendarmes coming.

"'I am very sorry for what has happened,' he says, 'but I'm obliged to make my report. I've just consulted my *Pocket Guide for the Gendarme*. There's an article in it against seditious emblems. Your fireworks comes under the law. You'll be prosecuted.'

"Prosecuted! We needed nothing but that! That capped the climax! But while I was wringing my hands, what do I see? Monsieur Cardinal's face lights up.

"'Make your report, my friend,' he says very softly to the sergeant, 'make your report!'

"Then he leads me aside.

"'A prosecution, Madame Cardinal, a political prosecution!—Why, it's a pedestal! I am saved!

My fortune is made. I will defend myself, because it's a downright swindle to hire a lawyer in such cases. The lawyer gets the whole benefit of the prosecution, makes a reputation over his client's back, and the client has to take the full penalty. And you have to pay the fellows, too, so that they get everything at once—money and honor. But they sha'n't have anything this time. I'll be my own lawyer! I'll begin this very night to prepare my defence.'

"And he's been working at his defence since day before yesterday. This is how it's going to begin:

"'Gentlemen, I meant to have some anticlerical fireworks; an unscrupulous manufacturer, who wanted to work off a lot of unseasonable goods, did not blush,' etc., etc.

"But he's beginning to be uneasy, because he hasn't seen anything of the summons.

"Every time the bell rings he rushes to the door and opens it himself:

"'There it is! It's my summons!'

"Alas! no, it's the butcher, or the baker, but not the summons.

"Monsieur Cardinal is in a fever, and just a minute ago, he said to me, in a bitter tone:

"'Don't they even mean to prosecute me?'

"Your old friend,

"ZOÉ CARDINAL."

My fortune is made. I will defend myself, because it's a downright swindle to hire a lawyer in such cases. The lawyer gets the whole benefit of the prosecution, makes a reputation over his client's back, and the client has to take the full penalty. And you have to pay the fellows, too, so that they get everything at once—money and honor. But they sha'n't have anything this time. I'll be my own lawyer! I'll begin this very night to prepare my

"Monsieur Cardinal is in a fever, and just a minute ago, he said to me, in a bitter tone:

" ' Don't they even mean to prosecute me ? '

"Your old friend,

"ZOÉ CARDINAL"

WS - #0162 - 020124 - C0 - 229/152/14 - PB - 9781333408176 - Gloss Lamination